The Reading Glass Books

1-888-420-3050
www.readingglassbooks.com
fulfillment@readingglassbooks.com

Table of Contents

This book of short stories is dedicated to all menopausal women:

There have been many books written about dating and how to meet men. The problem is that at this point in our lives, many of us have jiggly butts and sagging breasts and cannot compete with the youthful tight-ass, hard-body chicks, as my son refers to young, attractive women in the dating scene. We're more like aging hens waiting for the abattoir. We're not alone. There are a lot of us well-preserved, good-looking older cluckers who are searching for one more good lay in the hay.

We all have the same worries and fears. This book is about how four women have endured the aging process with some thoughts on how we got to where we are today based on childhood experiences.

Many thanks to the loyal friends that inspired me to write this book. The characters and stories are pure fiction and are built upon aging memories and newfound concerns of women who no longer have a twenty-one-inch waist.

We are the sharks!

Bitch, Lush, Slut, Princess Wannabe

One of my favorite songs of all time is "Get Over It" by the Eagles, and I believe that the only way a woman can deal with hitting fifty-five is to sing "Get Over It, Get Over It, Get Over It!" constantly to herself. Fifty was bad, but fifty-five is worse—it's almost sixty.

Well, several years ago, I read an article by an obviously male psychologist who maintained that the decade following the big four-oh kinda mellows you out, and you begin to feel comfortable with yourself. I have three significant friends who are like sisters, two developed on my own and one inherited by marriage. We're still trying to figure out if we were ever comfortable with ourselves, so the phrase "mellowing out" can be catalogued as more bullshit published in medical journals by psychologists and psychiatrists whose children had so many disorders they made your own little demons seem normal.

Every time in my life I was single, all of my friends were married. And at that time, our world revolved around children and couples and children and Trivial Pursuit and couples. The odd man out did not fit in to any of the above. Once you're fifty, that changes. Now life revolves around *us* and, for my friends, how they're going to knock me off so they can marry my husband. More on that subject later.

My name is Samantha Laraine Anderson. That is Laraine with an "a." I go by Laurie. My parents always called me Samantha Laraine. When I was in college, I called myself Laurel for a while, but one of the jocks kept referring to me and my roommate as Laurel and Hardy, so I went back to Laurie. My husband is Graham Jones.

After the third unsuccessful marriage, I quit changing my last name at the altar. Technically, Graham is my fifth attempt at marital bliss. I even did a repeat performance with number two—God knows why. He had many of the warning signs that should be part of the male evaluation phase in a potential relationship: bad in bed, cheap, abhorred physical exercise as noted fifteen years later by the fact he looks to be ten months pregnant with triplets, and completely lacked ambition. I married him the first time because I was consumed in law school debt.

Note, I did not say he was poor. Oh contraire. Cheap and rich often go together like oil and vinegar; however, cheap can easily be hidden during the courting phase of a relationship, especially when you're close to going over your personal fiscal cliff. Cheap is a trait that can easily be masked by a few expensive dinners and island holidays, so it's hard to uncover. I made the mistake the second time because I needed a paper in Advanced Tax Law. I was so desperate at that point I agreed to his demand of twenty BJs and me paying the airfare and hotel costs for a quickie marriage in Las Vegas. For that, he only got Circus Circus, not Caesar's Palace, and an Elvis drive-thru wedding. He kept a chalkboard in the family room to track payment on the debt.

Graham and I did abbreviated wedding vows and dropped the honor and obey crap and until death do us part. I sincerely believe this one is a keeper, but I don't want to take any chances. It should be noted that there was an asterisk in my vows that allowed me a one-night fling with Jim Palmer, in the event the potential presented itself. My affliction for "Cakes" will be discussed later in more detail.

Frances is my wacko, proper friend, and Sally CJ is my wacko-wacko friend. Marcia is my husband's sister who isn't wacko, just financially and white-knight-in-shining-armor deprived. Sometimes I think Frances is so proper and into Miss Manners that she sends a thank-you note to dates after a multi-climax night. Anyway, Frances is a natural beauty, size five, who thinks she's a fat pig and can't get laid for trying. Her wardrobe is impeccable and would make the late Jackie O proud. Sally CJ, on the other hand, is extremely well endowed, probably never wore a size five after three years of age, and gets laid routinely. Well, she admits to dry spells, but I don't think so. Sally CJ openly discusses my demise. Frances, being more proper, sits quietly by, waiting for the big day.

Inevitably, someone will ask how we met and got to be such good friends, and after looking at all the places we've each lived, it's amazing that our paths crossed. Frances and Sally CJ met at Converse College, a small girls' school in Spartanburg, South Carolina, where girls were allowed to bring their horses and were taught all the fine arts of becoming a southern lady. Frances went there because she always wanted to learn how to ride and hoped to make friends with a horse owner; Sally CJ picked the school because it was a warm climate and far away from home.

Bits of the southern-lady and finishing-school type of stuff stuck with Frances, but Sally CJ hated every second of living in the South and vowed never to live below the Mason-Dixon Line. Following graduation, she fled the South and moved to Boston. She moved to Pittsburgh when she married Al, the party animal. I met Sally CJ when Graham and I moved to Pittsburgh for a brief period. She immediately introduced me to Frances, who apparently grew up in the Burgh. She returned to her childhood hometown because she was convinced she could parlay her college-acquired southern drawl to charm the men she grew up with—men who were known for saying things like, "Yinz guys goin' dahntahn n'at?" and "How 'baut dem Stillers?" Needless to say, she's still trying.

The three of us lived in the Burgh for only a few years since our careers have had us moving around like vagabonds. At the present time, we're scattered across the country. I live in Las Vegas, Sally CJ just moved from New Jersey back to Boston in search of a better dating pool, Frances splits her time between DC and Pittsburgh, and Marcia is enjoying the rays in Hilton Head. Thank God for frequent-flier miles.

I have made it clear to Graham that if he as much as thinks about sleeping with either Sally CJ or Frances when I die, Ambien will not help his sleep patterns. Fortunately, Marcia is not interested in a sexual relationship with her brother. She's just looking for a mirror image of her sibling without any matching DNA.

You may think I'm exaggerating. Not. Last year I was sitting at a tennis match in San Diego waiting for Serena Williams to beat the shit out of Maria Sharapova when I decided to call Sally CJ and, acting cool in front of all the rich La Jolla snots who were listening to every word spoken during my cell phone conversation while they drooled over Graham and tried to figure out what soap he was starring in, invited her to join Graham and me during our vacation at our private villa (Ha! Ha!) in Bermuda. I just can't get this texting shit down. I think it's the nails, but I'm so techno-challenged. I see seventy-year-old women who can't even see and six-year-old children who can't spell texting. Maybe that's my problem. I can spell, so BFF, LOL, POS (oops, know that one) are not in my lingo.

After all, we were going to be there for two weeks and why did we need a two-bedroom cottage for the two of us? We had our bed, a living room couch, the kitchen counter, the dining room table, the patio chaise lounge, and the shower for sexual encounters; another bed would be superfluous. It was an honest and sincere offer. She accepted. Period.

One thing about the girls, we do not communicate very well. Our word is our bond. "I'll be there," spoken during our abbreviated cell phone conversation meant *I'll find a flight and e-mail you what time I'll arrive, so you better have meant the invite or you'll be sorry.* Two days later, Sally CJ sent me an e-mail that read: USAir flight 190, September 4 at 1:30 p.m.

That was it.

The following month, Graham and I arrived in Bermuda and spent five days scuba diving and playing golf and trying new sex positions and working on increasing our alcohol tolerance in anticipation of the arrival of Sally CJ. We went to the local liquor store and bought a fifth of Grey Goose, three bottles of red wine, a half-gallon of Black Seal Rum, and some generic gin for Graham. We were ready.

The girls are self-sufficient. She knew where we were staying. We waited. And we waited. Two hours after her flight was due to arrive, we were still waiting. Something was wrong.

The concierge at the club where we stayed knew the airport manager for US Air. There was no Sally CJ MacAllister on the flight manifest. We asked ourselves, was she really coming? After all, we never really spoke to her about travel arrangements. Had the Internet failed us? Did she get thrown off the flight? Did she try to smuggle illegal contraband on the plane and get caught, only to be sitting in jail in Philly waiting to get raped by some dyke? Let me tell you—that would not be acceptable to Sally CJ. Men yes, girls never.

We were panicked. I called her office phone. No answer.

I called her house. No answer.

I called her office again and pushed the pound key to speak to someone.

"Hello."

"May I speak to Sally CJ MacAllister, please?"

"Shin's not in," was the response.

"Is shin not in because you think shin's in Bermuda?" I adapt to the language translation very well.

"Oh no, I knew shin left the office too late …"

That's right. Sally CJ was sitting on Interstate 476, watching the big blue and gray bird fly off to Bermuda without her. I called her cell phone and was greeted by, "Yeah? I'm fucking pissed. I'm getting drunk at the beach at Atlantic City. I missed my fucking flight. I'll be there tomorrow."

Click.

Dead silence.

The bitch hung up on me. I didn't have the chance to say I was pissed or that I was worried that she was getting raped in a Philadelphia jail. I didn't get to say that I missed three hours of prime beach time waiting for her sorry ass. No, she pulled the perfect power trip. "Missed my flight, see you tomorrow." Click.

Immediately, I muttered, "You slut, you met a hunk and blew me off for a day at the Jersey shore."

Twenty-four hours later, we took a taxi to the airport and were there to greet the sorry bitch as she sashayed out the front door, followed by two porters in apparent heat. We even had drinks to make it back to the cottage. After all, a fifteen-minute ride to your accommodations when you're already a day late starting your vacation mandates immediate alcohol nourishment.

The next four days were a blur. They were great. By Friday, the liquor was gone. If you licked the sweat off our arms (not that a normal person would want to do this), you could get drunk. It was luxurious.

We were working on doing a semi-dry-out at one of the pools before Sally CJ's flight home. She was planning my funeral and her immediate wedding to Graham. She decided that the most appropriate and cost-effective approach would be to have a joint funeral-wedding. After all, the attendees would pretty much be the same.

Graham didn't say a word other than to offer encouragement in her fantasy plan. I looked suspiciously at the rum and Diet Coke she so kindly brought me from the condo.

It was a brilliant plan and there was no one at the pool to overhear the conniving and planning for the early termination of my life.

Come to think of it, whenever the girls are at a pool, there's never anyone else around.

Not to divert from my imminent death, but this reminds me of the trip to Puerto Vallarta. Graham nervously bid me good-bye one Memorial Day weekend for a girls-only week in Puerto Vallarta. We departed from three different cities—Las Vegas, Pittsburgh, and Philly—and coordinated our flights so we would all arrive in Puerto Vallarta around two o'clock in the afternoon. That way we could all share a taxi to the hotel. I knew we did *not* want Sally CJ loose in a foreign country without chaperones.

I had just claimed my bags from the carousel when Frances poked me in the ribs. Perfect timing. She looked like she walked off the runway modeling the latest spring collection for Versace.

"Are those Christian Louboutin's you're wearing? This is Mexico, not the Rivera," I said as I looked at my not too chic sundress and matching Dr. Scholl's.

"You never know. Where's the slut?"

We schlepped our bags to the arrivals board and noted that there were three flights from Philadelphia; one arrived two hours earlier, one was canceled, and one was due in after dinner.

We looked at each other and shook our heads in unison. "This isn't a good start. If she was on that canceled flight, Lord knows what she'll do and when she'll arrive, if at all. It's going to be a very long night waiting for her, so we might as well take a taxi to the hotel and try to call her when we get there to find out her flight arrangements."

"You're right. We might as well enjoy our beach time." If Sally CJ was booked on the canceled flight and had to spend five hours in the US Air lounge, pity the flight crew and us when she finally touched down in Mexico.

So Frances and I grabbed a taxi and headed to the Westin Regina. The WR is a very upscale resort with the cutest Mexican wait-staff in the world, and by the time Frances and I arrived, Sally CJ was already there, knew most of them on a first name basis, and had upgraded our rooms to beachfront, with a Jacuzzi on the porch.

"Where have you been? I've been here for almost two hours. Fortunately I arrived at the airport early only to find out that my flight was canceled. After telling the ticketing agent that I was meeting my best friends in the world in Mexico to grieve my recent husband's death, I found myself in the first-class cabin surrounded by sympathetic flight attendants who kept serving me vodka tonics to drown my sorrows."

"Al isn't dead. And you've been divorced for seven years."

"Yeah, he's alive, but one can always hope. I still hate that bastard."

Then she proceeded to make introductions to the boys who had been primed to bring us *cervezas* to help get us up to speed.

Rigioberto was mine, Roberto serviced (oops, served) Sally CJ, and Jorge tended to Frances. I suspect that Jorge would have liked to have done a lot more tending than Frances permitted. I had to give the guy credit; he never gave up trying to win her affection up to the minute we checked out of the hotel and got in the taxi to return to the airport.

The same is true of the professional soccer player I picked up for her in a dance contest. I thought he was kinda cute, but Frances blew him off before he could say his name was Joe.

I should have killed her on the spot for my personal humiliation. The final dance-off was to "Let's Twist Again" by Chubby Checker, and I was out there doing the United States proud—boobs swaying and cellulite jiggling, not even thinking about a Janet Jackson wardrobe malfunction, reliving the twist contest I was in at Friday Night Assembly in tenth grade. I was in the twist finals with Jimmy Wilcox when my blue chiffon dress began disintegrating. First the belt flew off. Then the sides started to part. I already had a huge run in my right stocking, and my pink garter belt was slipping down my butt.

This time it was an aging Laurie against a nineteen-year-old beach volleyball hard body whose body parts (both real and augmented) stayed firmly in place. I'm sure that later that evening there was a crowd watching videos on someone's cell phone in the bar. Thank God it didn't go viral on YouTube. I had no idea what was being said in the bar because my Spanish isn't that good, but I thought I heard, *"Ballena varada,"* and I wasn't aware of any beached whale sightings on the coast of Mexico.

Oh well.

All that, and Frances was not receptive to my dance partner's advances. Maybe it was when he took off his Yankees baseball cap, and she noticed that he was a candidate for Rogaine. I wonder if there's been a study to see if men who wear baseball hats more than twelve hours a day have a greater propensity for baldness. Or maybe, who wants to get laid by a guy who wears a Yankees baseball cap?

There are five pools at the WR, one of which was ours. It took us two days to lay claim, but after that, no one else dared venture near. We were the three killer sharks in the water, swimming with our menacing hand-fin in the air, judiciously guarding the swim-up bar, baring our breasts at women who gave us dirty looks, and zealously making sure that no one had the opportunity to lounge in the decadent pool beds.

Now, back to the pending end of my life. Even without the assistance of Frances, we were able to take control of the pool at the club in Bermuda. Graham was just an innocent bystander. Potential widower and newlywed, yet innocent bystander.

What made it worse was that I was prepared to die. I had injured my back and could not sit for more than two minutes. I needed drugs and had none, and I was afraid to take what Sally CJ was offering me. I figured that death was a preferred alternative to the twelve-hour flight to the West Coast.

Sally CJ agreed.

Graham was a little too quiet.

I did not drink the Diet Coke.

Sally CJ is still my best friend.

Graham is still my loving husband.

Life at fifty-five is great.

> *I think every woman is entitled to a middle
> husband she can forget.*
>
> *—Adela Rogers St. John*

Growing Old Gracefully

Whoever coined the phrase "growing old gracefully" was a lonely, ugly woman who never had a date in high school and was waiting until mid-age to finally snare the quarterback on her high school football team. Obviously, the statement's originator was not the high school prom queen or the head of the cheerleading squad.

No woman over fifty who has any self-respect or pride can stand in the front of her bathroom mirror and say that she's genuinely happy to look like Mrs. Milhoag, her high school English teacher, affectionately referred to as Mrs. Warthog, who could have been the twin sister of your neighbor's Shar-Pie. Remember, she was the teacher whose jowls flapped like a bat taking off when she turned her head trying to catch that creep, Jimmy Wilkowski, throw the spitball across the room at his true love, Susan Brzezinski. Remember, the one with the sagging jowls and puffy eyes whose body was so juicy that even if Spanx had been invented back then she still couldn't squeeze into a size eighteen dress?

I can actually handle the sagging breasts and the cellulite that come with the aging process because you can cover them up with Escada and St. John clothing, and no one will be the wiser. In fact, women are jealous because you look so in-vogue. In-vogue. That's the code word for clothes that are so expensive and the material so thick and luxurious that no one focuses on the ripples of cellulite underneath.

Let's face it, there aren't enough hours in the day to work, cook dinner, make sure your teenage children aren't in jail, and exercise a sufficient number of hours to burn off the cookies and chocolate bars so you can look like Catherine Zeta-Jones. Something has to go, so obviously, what you can't see, no one will know is wrinkled.

Even my husband noticed when my favorite pastime became standing in front of the bathroom mirror pulling the skin back so I could see my heart-shaped jaw line. I think I read in *Cosmo* that those of us blessed with a heart shaped face are the first to go because for forty-plus years, you're used to that ugly, pointed chin, and then one day you get up and look in the mirror—and shazam, your face looks like a square.

After doses of cold water and making sure you don't have Alzheimer's, you're satisfied that yes, it's you, and yes, you did have a heart-shaped face, and yes, that is loose skin hanging there making your face look like a basset hound. The sure sign of aging is when you keep a scotch tape dispenser in the bathroom. That's right, I used to scotch tape my face back, but all it did was create a strawberry-blonde oriental look that wasn't very becoming and resulted in the loss of more precious hair when I ripped the tape off in disgust.

The girls aren't ecstatic about aging either. Marcia has always vowed that she's ready to undergo the knife the very instant a plastic surgeon is ready to cut and there's a funding source with $15,000 of ready cash. Hey, guys, unlock your wallet! Just think of all those frequent flyer miles you can earn by lending Marcia your Platinum Visa. And, as a bonus, you can date a hot chick without jowls.

Sally CJ believes that sex is the magic elixir for all evils. How can you disagree as long as the men keep coming? Her thirty-four double Ds don't seem to be getting any smaller with age. Men never seem to get to her face when they look at her.

Frances, on the other hand, has expressed a lot more self-restraint, probably because she watched one of the medical shows of an actual facelift on the Learning Channel. I've noticed that her wine cooler recently increased in size, and there seems to be a rapid rotation of bottles. She's approaching aging through wine and high-price face creams on the premise that a permanent wine buzz is better than the pain of working out.

Several years ago, there was an article in the *Washingtonian* magazine that showed photographs of a facelift and described the process in excruciating detail, as well as the accompanying pain that was associated with the urge to regain one's youth. That article suggested that growing old gracefully had some merit. I saved it just in case I needed to be reminded about how low my pain threshold actually is.

I don't do too well with pain. That was the reason I went to the doctor for the terrible sciatica I suffered when I used to run. I found in my twenties and thirties that running was a great way to meet guys that didn't have guts and flabby breasts—guys that liked to drink beer and party and didn't want to look like Archie Bunker when they hit middle age.

I actually tried to train for a marathon but couldn't get past the ten-mile marker. That was okay. I looked great, and men were always impressed when I said I ran and wanted to run a marathon before I hit thirty. So I lied. No fact checkers around here. The story still works when I say the same thing about running a marathon before I turn sixty. Fortunately, no one ever called my bluff and wanted to start the grueling training program for the Marine Corps Marathon that's published every year in the *Washington Post*.

The goal of running 26.2 miles at one time actually ended before I hit thirty, when I became pregnant with my son. I did manage to run for seven months of my pregnancy. Thank God I did, because I gained more than sixty-five pounds when I was pregnant and dread to think how many pounds I would have gained if I just sat on my ass thinking about the pain I was going to go through during the birthing process.

The fear of giving birth grew as my belly expanded, and then one day when I was waddling from the train at the Farragut Square Metro stop, I saw Randy Brown. Actually, his name is Morgan Arthur Randolph Philip Brown. Obviously, his parents couldn't focus and had a naming issue. Maybe that's one of the reasons he was diagnosed with adult ADD. I had a massive crush on him in high school, along with almost every other girl in my graduation class, but Randy wound up marrying prissy Joyce Garland.

Joyce Garland and I went all the way through school together from first grade, and most of the time, we were really good friends. We were usually elected to some class office and did all the right social activities—you know, honor society, Friday night ballroom dancing, girl scouts, piano lessons—but Joyce was the girl who was prim and proper, and I was the jock and class clown.

I can still remember the Halloween party at Ann Hall's house in tenth grade. We had to dress up, and I obsessed with snaring Randy Brown with my sexy costume. Picture Laurie dressed up as a cannibal— black leotard and tights, with white fringes from my mother's kitchen mop draped around my midsection, one of my dog's gnawed-on plastic turkey drumsticks at the top of my ponytail, and black streaks covering the acne that the Stridex didn't wipe out in time for the big event. I was one hot number for sure.

Then, Joyce walked in the room dressed as Cinderella in a white flowing gown and, I swear, glass slippers. (In retrospect, they were probably plastic.) At that instant, I knew that the only thing my lips were going to be touching that night was the fake turkey bone I was gnawing on.

Yeah, I guess in retrospect I understand why I lost out that night. I never felt quite the same toward Joyce after that, but it wasn't her fault. Her mother was aware of the true difference between a fairy princess and cannibal, and my mother was lacking in traditional feminine qualities. Although both are man-eating, Joyce's mother was just a little more subtle and understood that the term should not be taken literally.

Anyway, I got off the train at the Farragut Square Metro stop and was heading to a meeting with three lawyers who offered nothing for fantasy fucking. You know the type—pudgy, balding, parents refused to get them braces in junior high. It was one of those hot, humid, miserable Washington, DC, afternoons … the kind of day when your pantyhose are instantly soaking wet and cling in your crack, so you walk with the tighten-your-ass wiggle-waggle-push-push trying to free them.

Someone from a cool, dry climate not familiar with the movement might think your Tampax was slipping out and you were trying to compress your vaginal muscles to keep it from falling on the sidewalk. I knew there was a reason why my mom insisted on underwear.

Yes, I still wear pantyhose. Francis keeps telling me to get with it, but I hate underpants. Thongs get stuck in my butt crack and are so uncomfortable. Maybe some women like the feel of something stuck in one's crack, and that's how thongs were invented. I prefer the alternative solution, as only a lawyer would say, briefs *de minimis*, i.e., bare ass. Besides, pantyhose hide cellulite.

Anyway, there was Randy Brown going up the escalator. I hadn't seen Randy since high school when we sat in English class and tried to see who could hold quarters longer in our Hercules belly button. If my son tried to do that today in high school, he would be suspended for at least a week.

Well, Randy still looked great and had graduated from the Naval Academy and was still married to the Priss and was going to start medical school in the spring and had four wonderful and adorable kids who were perfect, and his life was wonderful and close to Ozzie and Harriet, and would I like to bring my husband to their house for dinner that Friday night because he knew Joyce would love to see me. Wow, my juices were still flowing after all these years. It was encouraging that I could still get a rush when I was fat and pregnant!

Sure Joyce would like to see me. She probably looked great, and I looked like a water buffalo, but what the heck. I had pretty much gotten over the Cinderella night. We went to dinner and met their wonderfully behaved kids—who had names like Muffy, Buffy, and Fluffy, and some other clever name like Cottontail—and had a delightful time reminiscing about high school and growing up.

I then admitted my fear of the pain associated with childbirth, and Joyce told me there was nothing to worry about. "Having babies," Joyce ever so wisely pontificated, "is nothing more than having your body work with you in a glorious natural event."

Fuck that shit. After twenty-six hours of grueling labor, I knew I should have hired an assassin after that Halloween party in tenth grade. I didn't take Lamaze classes, and when one of my college dorm mates turned out to be the birthing room nurse, she got the picture really fast that I wasn't going to look at that goddamned heart on the ceiling and make pathetic panting noises like some aborigine while my body worked with me in a glorious manner with nature.

I ran into Joyce a couple years ago at our high school reunion. She was talking with one of the members of her snotty, prissy click from twelfth grade, and tears were streaming down her cheeks.

"We moved to San Diego, and Randy was working a lot of hours in the surgical unit. I knew he seemed to be tired all the time and was worried that he was working himself to the point of exhaustion. Then one day he came home and said he was leaving for a tour in Hawaii with one of the surgical nurses. And before I knew it, he was gone. Twenty-five years of marriage, then poof!"

This is an area of my expertise, but I didn't know how to tell Joyce that a husband who works long hours and is physically exhausted is probably dipping his wick somewhere else, of which I have been the lucky recipient on numerous occasions. I just shook my head in an understanding manner while my fist was clenched and I muttered, "Yes!" to myself.

I hate to admit it, but I actually felt sorry for her because she had lived such a fairytale life and had no clue what most of us suffered through growing up. Best of all, she admitted that Randy left her with a true legacy: Muffy (or was it Buffy?) had ADD with hyperactivity. Paybacks are hell.

Anyway, back to running, sciatica, and pain. When I went to the doctor to find out what to do about my lower back pain, I casually asked him about my bunions. He X-rayed my back and feet and came in a little while later and said, "There's good news, and there's bad news. The good news is that you don't need back surgery."

Back surgery, fuck me, I never thought that was an option. I just wanted some drugs so I could get back to running again and maybe have a few out-of-body experiences as a side benefit.

"But," he continued, "you do need surgery for bunions, and I suggest that we do a bilateral McBride bunionectomy.

"See that protrusion? What I'll do is file that growth off. Then, in order to realign the digits, I'll make an incision here and cut the tendon, then cast the foot. I'd be prepared to be completely immobile for at least two weeks. I can write an authorization for you to miss three weeks of work."

"I doubt that will be necessary."

"I strongly recommend that we do both feet at the same time, but of course, the final decision is up to you."

I thought I said we should take it slow. In retrospect, I think he heard, "That's a go."

I do remember that he gave me some mumbo jumbo that sometimes it's better to get it over with all at once rather than going through the recovery twice. Notice, there was no mention of the word "pain." I walked out of his office with a prescription for a muscle relaxer for my back and with the knowledge that Dr. Davis was going to remove the bunion from my right foot and that I would be back at the office in a week.

Dr. Davis gave me the names of other orthopedic surgeons for a second opinion, which was required by my insurance company.

I went to Dr. Johnson and filled out sixteen thousand inane medical forms and other papers regarding my medical problems. Stuff like, *When did you have your last DPT shot?* I had to draw on a paper with feet what surgery was proposed for which he was to provide a second opinion. I drew a huge bunion on the right foot and handed him the medical opinion prepared by my surgeon. He looked at my rendering like a mother looks at the drawing made by her preschool child with this quizzical look on his face.

He smiled politely and asked how my feet were, and I said that I had a hard time squeezing into my stilettos. He suggested that flat-heeled shoes were probably in my future and concurred with Dr. Davis's recommendation for a bilateral McBride bunionectomy.

Two weeks later, I woke up in the Point Park Surgical Unit and was distressed to see both of my feet in casts. Despite the fact that I'm relatively educated and an attorney, I didn't make the connection that bilateral meant two. At that moment, I understood why Dr. Johnson had that strange look on his face when he looked at my artist sketch of the pending surgery.

My husband wheeled me out to the car and lifted me into the front seat, and then I knew that I was not going to be back at work in a week's time. Apparently, so did everyone at work because they figured out what the term bilateral meant and didn't share that intimate secret with me.

Well, the next day, after the pain medicine from the surgery wore off, I understood that Joyce was right. Having a baby was nothing. My body was clearly not working with me on either foot. In fact, my body was rebelling profusely against the removal of part of the bone that had begun to protrude on my foot like a sixth toe.

The lesson was clear. A child obviously was not meant by God to be a permanent attachment, but a growth on your foot is meant to be part of your foot as a sixth digit. Amen.

It's a good thing that Dr. Davis tricked me and did the bilateral job because I would never have returned for the left foot.

The repeated use of the word *pain* in the *Washingtonian* article on facelifts worked like a charm for several years. Obviously, time dilutes the memory of pain. Some women have more children to get additional food stamps, some want to maximize their tax deductions, and others are plain stupid. You would have to pay me a six-digit number to serve as a surrogate mother, and even then, I'd have to think about the proposition very seriously. Nature apparently has a way of convincing women how cute and cuddly babies are, and we foolishly forget the pain in giving birth, intentionally forget to take our birth control pill, and consequently have more children.

Well, my son was not particularly cuddly. In fact, he cried 90 percent of the time from 10:00 p.m. to 2:00 a.m., which made waking up for work at 5:00 in the morning a living hell. So I never let myself forget what a liar Joyce was. Pain is something that I make considerable effort to avoid, until I look in the mirror every morning.

Finally one day, I got fed up with the morning mirror routine and made a joint appointment for my husband and I to meet with a cosmetic surgeon for a consultation on the avenues that were available for us to reduce the aging process. When you walk in the office, it's impossible not to notice that everyone who works there is beautiful. I guess it would be bad for business for a cosmetic surgeon whose logo includes a picture of Venus de Milo to be surrounded by ugly people, but it's very depressing anyway.

Immediately, I blurted out, "Is that really you or did Dr. Taylor help you along?"

What are they supposed to say? "Oh, my, I used to look like I got hit in the face with a bag of nickels, and then I met Dr. T."

"No," she said. "Dr. T. is really good. He can even make you look younger." The "you" was about six syllables in length and spoken in an extended southern drawl.

Great. Good thing the consultation had been prepaid or I woulda been gone. How dare she imply that I needed cosmetic surgery!

Well, Dr. Taylor was a cross between Marcus Welby and Phil Donohue, and I loved him immediately. After having lines drawn all over our faces to demonstrate the level of work we needed to look like the receptionist, I offered Graham up as the sacrificial lamb to have his eyes debagged. He wasn't interested.

After a brief overview of the pricing, I indicated that maybe I could have my eyes done now and then get a total facelift in a couple of years. Dr. Taylor declined and told me to come back after I hit the Megabucks jackpot. His assessment was that just doing my eyes would only draw more attention to one of my three chins and that I wouldn't be very happy with the results.

Ever since we moved to the gaming capital of the nation, I abandoned my love of slot machines, so it didn't look like there was much hope for me to be surgically enhanced. As soon as Graham left town the next day, I made an appointment for his eyes to be done. I thought it would be a lovely Christmas gift for him instead of the routine gifts he got like bedroom slippers, ties, and oh yeah, steak knives. This showed that I really cared.

I kind of viewed this as a family project. If Graham turned out okay and could handle the pain, then I would go ahead with the Megabucks process. If he had too much pain, I would continue to invest in every age-defying face cream sold to mankind and continue with the scotch tape routine. Much to my amazement, Graham was not too pleased with my aggressive move.

When the nurse called him to schedule his blood work and pre-op procedures, he politely declined and booked me for the full frontal and scheduled my pre-op procedures.

He called me and left a message on my cell phone, "Checkmate."

When I played the message back, I couldn't figure out what "checkmate" meant. Then Miss Beautiful from Dr. T's office called and advised me that I had an appointment the next day for blood work for my upcoming facelift. I should have been overjoyed.

The phone rang again. My blood boiled as I glanced at the caller ID. "This is what you wanted. You just used me as a pawn, and I countered your move. You're under the knife next week, honey. Merry Christmas."

I called the girls to let them know that I was outfoxed by a man. That was the most embarrassing part. I couldn't even think of the upcoming pain without being pissed that my husband outmaneuvered me at my own game.

The next week went by too fast, and the next thing I knew, I was sitting by the back door of Dr. Taylor's surgical unit waiting to be wheeled out by my husband. I now understand why they never wheel you out through the reception area; it wouldn't be good for business. Graham walked in the room and let out the most blood-curdling scream you've ever heard. It was a scene from the *Exorcist*. I wasn't exactly a candidate for Miss America.

I was wrapped in a black shroud with tape around my head that made it look like a football helmet. There were two little peepholes for my eyes and a hole for my mouth. This wasn't going to be a good

Christmas, but I smiled as I realized that I could get rid of the scotch tape dispenser in the bathroom. I know Graham was contemplating getting me a burka for an early Christmas gift with maybe some sexy little La Perla underpinnings.

Obviously, grace is not one of my attributes.

*I have reached the age where competence
is a turn on.*

—Billy Joel

A Sensual Prune

Have you ever seen a sensual prune? You say, "Fool, prunes are not sensual." Well, that's just my point. The basic facts of nature are the same for fruit and women. Take a nice juicy plum, add a few summers at the beach, and what do you have? Voila, a dried up, old prune—exactly what I see in the mirror every morning.

I tried to explain this concept to Frances a couple months ago, and it took a long time to get her to see the point. You see, Frances finally ended a relationship that had been going nowhere for the past eight years and was getting the urge, if you know what I mean. She has a terrific career, no kids from a previous marriage as baggage, drives a flashy red Corvette convertible, and has the taste of Ivana Trump. The only problem is that she has the net worth of Sister Mary Katherine at the local convent.

I think Frances is the reason why websites like guilt.com, therealreal. com, hautelook.com, shopedropoff.com, and snobswap.com were invented. They enable normal people who relate to the Little Sisters of the Poor to look like they live and shop in Manhattan.

Anyway, Frances lives in Pittsburgh, which is also the location of our hairdresser. That's right. I fly 2,066 miles to get a haircut every six weeks. Fortunately, I have a business client in Pittsburgh whom I have convinced needs to meet with me on monthly basis. It's too difficult to go through the hassle of finding a new hairdresser, which I'm sure you can understand. My husband, on the other hand, being a male, is not as swift and cannot understand why there are no hairdressers in Las Vegas who can dye my hair the correct shade of strawberry blonde. I tried to convince him that Frank Woods has this special product that won't bleach out in the sun and that he refuses to share the formula with any potential competitor in Las Vegas. Yeah, my husband hasn't bought that one either.

To men, a haircut is a haircut is a haircut, and they don't understand all of the special intimacies a woman has with her hairdresser. Actually, my client is also wise to my mandate to meet with him on a monthly basis; however, he tolerates it because I never charge for a hotel room, and he finally met Frances and thinks she's hot.

Anyway, the last time I was in Pittsburgh, Frances innocently asks—while we were dining on a low-fat spinach and dried tomato pasta salad accompanied by a loaf of French bread with garlic butter, and of course, a dietetic glass of Graves—"Tell me why I shouldn't sleep with this guy in my office who's six foot three, has the body of Adonis, looks like Antonio Banderas, and is definitely interested?"

After choking on my wine, I wince and ask, "What's the catch?"

Obviously, there's a catch, or she wouldn't have been sitting there with a stupid grin on her face and would have started the discussion by saying something more definitive like, "Guess what?"

"He's also handy around the house and offered to show me how to use the drill I just bought that has interchangeable bits."

Now I know we're in trouble. Frances isn't the handy-woman type and definitely not the type to go into Home Depot to purchase any type of mechanical device. The Pleasure Chest, yes. Home Depot or Lowes, a resounding no! And now she's using words like interchangeable drill bits. I take another sip of wine and begin to stare her down.

Oh, yeah, did I forget to mention that Frances bought a wonderful turn-of-the-century Victorian house in a neat neighborhood where everyone has performed gorgeous renovations and that her house has this wonderful porch where we like to dine and read Neiman Marcus catalogues and that, by the way, she got a really good deal on her house because she bought it "as is" from another woman who also has a great shoe collection …

Anyway, Frances finally indicated that there might be a slight complication. "He's married," she blurted out. I continued the stare-down because I knew there was more to the problem than a wedding band.

"Oh, all right, he's married and has two young children and loves his wife, and he's twenty-six years old."

Now we have finally arrived at the heart of the matter. He's twenty-six years old and wants to have an intimate relationship with my best friend who's on the backside of fifty. I'm outraged.

Here I am spending all my spare time slathering new rejuvenating products containing various forms of alpha hydroxyl on my face to firm and miraculously remove the new wrinkles that seem to show up each day as the plum-to-prune transformation continues to take effect, and a twenty-six-year-old Adonis wants to sleep with my best friend. I ask the first pertinent question. "Why?"

Now there are lots of ways to ask, "Why?" and I had to make certain "why" sounded like "Why would *you* want to get involved" and not "Why would a twenty-six-year-old Adonis want to sleep with *you?*" After all, no twenty-six-year-old Adonis has been knocking on my door, and I spent an entire Christmas holiday looking like a ghoul, so I might be a little jealous, but Frances is my best friend, and she once told me that she never dressed like Cinderella for Halloween parties when she was in high school. I believed her. Bitch.

I remember years ago when Frances and I read Terry McMillan's book, *How Stella Got Her Groove Back,* so I had to tactfully find out if she was fantasizing. I heard that there are some side effects from one of the newer antiaging facial creams that's only available by mail order, which I happened to see in Frances's medicine cabinet. Frances had a previous cougar fling, but that was when she was thirty-nine, and the guy was twenty-five. She's always on the cutting edge of new trends, but fifty-five and twenty-six? I don't think so.

"How do you know he wants to sleep with you? Maybe he's just being helpful."

Frances snidely replied, "I told him I that would bring my drill to the office, and he said he could get a better feel and check the snugness of fittings if we worked on it together at my house."

I think she ran out and opened up a Home Depot charge account and purchased every power tool in stock.

She's right, the boy is hot. But she didn't ask me how to seduce him. She asked why she shouldn't sleep with him. Good sign. That's maturity. "Well, you should never sleep with someone you work with," I responded with a slight tinge of disgust in my voice. Yeah right, you know that's bullshit. Okay, so I met my current husband at the office. In fact, after divorcing my high school sweetheart, my next marriages were all work-related fatalities. And that's not even thinking about the affairs I don't want to be reminded of. Office relationships were the major reason I had to change jobs so often.

"He's probably just using you to get ahead," I said with utmost confidence.

"Yep, I'm sure of it," she responded. "Isn't that what Mary Cunningham did when she was our role model in the eighties?"

Oh yeah, I forgot about good old Mary Cunningham and Bill Agee. Built one hell of a national reputation in holding down the front office. Good role model. Interesting, no one calls Bill Clinton a role model, and he was president of the United States. People were so accepting of JFK, but beyond that, men's infidelities have been viewed as disgusting, yet they never stop making headline news. Tisk. Tisk.

"He loves his wife and has babies," I said with great indignation.

"I didn't say I wanted to marry him or adopt his kids. It's just a temporary solution to this persistent problem, like I haven't been laid since New Year's Eve, and it's now September."

That's a tough one to respond to, based on the original directive of convincing her why she shouldn't sleep with the most gorgeous man she claims we've ever known.

Then it hit me. "Sure he knows what you look like on the outside, and he's obviously mesmerized by your charm and grace and designer clothes, but are you going to do it with the lights on or off? Missionary position? Because if you're going to do it with the lights even dimly lit with you on top, he'll know that you're no longer a plum, and when it's all over, he'll always look at like you like you're aging fruit."

That did it.

We agreed that if and when he approached her again, she would go shopping for shoes. Not underwear, not power tools. Shoes.

I never married because I have three pets at home that answer the same purpose as a husband. I have a dog that growls every morning, a parrot that swears all afternoon, and a cat that comes home late at night.

—Marie Corelli

Up, Up, and Away and PCOT

I spend more than 80 percent of my life on the road. Yeah, I'm one of those business travelers that the airlines in their desperate financial condition are supposed to be sucking up to. That's a real crock of shit if I ever heard one.

I travel pretty routinely to Sunnyvale, California, and fly in and out of San Francisco airport. I tried San Jose and Southwest Airlines (the airline for people without a purpose in life), but by the time I waited for forty-five minutes in line for the fourth time—you know, baggage check-in, security check-in, seat check-in, line up like cattle going to slaughter, and then boarding check-in—I was ready to check someone out. Then the giggly teenage flight attendant with shorts and sneakers and perky breasts threw a bag of peanuts at me and exclaimed, "Bad hands! Hope you're not playin' for the Giants tonight!" I jumped up to smack her but forgot my seatbelt was tightly strapped across my lap and almost lost the lower part of my body. Bitch. Anyway, that's why I only fly the friendly skies of United.

Believe me. There are no friendly skies. One day, I finished up at the office early and thought I could catch the 6:20 flight back home. In order to determine whether or not I should run everyone off Highway 101 in order to accomplish this objective, I called the airline to see if the flight was full. "Wide open, ma'am," was what I was told. I was off. Traffic was minimal since it was a clear Thursday night, and I made it to the rental car return without causing one person to play the good old middle-finger game with me. I even got to apply a little mascara, eyeliner, and lipstick as I swerved in and out of cars.

Would you believe that a town council outside Cleveland has pending legislation to outlaw applying mascara while driving? Cell phones and texting are one thing, but mascara? Come now. Do those people have such a dull life in the Midwest that they're able to accomplish applying makeup at home in front of a mirror in the morning? Or maybe they just don't multitask well. They probably iron their underwear also. Amazing.

In fact, not only do they want to outlaw applying makeup while driving, they want to outlaw eating and drinking in the car. I do not mean alcohol. I mean beverages like coffee in the morning. I figure someone should send that proposal to the automakers, and they can put the kibosh on that nonsense pretty quick. After all, how much money has Ford and GM invested in cup holders?

Anyway, I made it through security in fifteen minutes, thanks to the Premier line, and ran to the gate ticket counter. Whenever I run through an airport, I still think of OJ and those old Hertz commercials. Then I think of OJ and the feat he accomplished in the California court system. Whatever happed to Marcia Clark? Shit. When I fuck up, I get fired. Other people like Marcia Clark who let a killer get away with murder become movie stars and wind up rich.

The monitor said the flight was boarding. I was going to be home early. Oh boy. As I rushed up to the ticket counter, this snarly-looking goat with half-rim bifocals looked up and said, "Are you Johnson?"

I replied, "No, I'm Anderson."

The PMS goat just glared. Did I do that bad a job putting on my mascara and lipstick in the car? Guess I should I have said, "No, I'm Laurie Anderson, 100K flyer, lover of the friendly skies, the kind of person you should be sucking up to so you can continue to work in a job that requires customer service."

I decided it was wise to keep such thoughts to myself and politely asked if there were any seats available so I could get home early to see my husband. This was a no-brainer question since I already knew that the plane was wiiiiiide open. "Sorry, the flight is full," the PMS goat hissed at me.

"You lying, lazy, ugly piece of shit," I muttered to myself. Maturity is a wonderful blessing. So is the fact that my husband was in Chicago, and I wasn't going to get laid if I got home at eight or ten. "Oh, shucks, I guess fifty people who didn't have confirmed seats managed to check in within the last hour. Must have been a high school football team that finished up early. Huh?"

Deadpan face on the woman. I think she dipped her head lower so her snarl over the glasses was increased. "Pardon me?"

"I said, yes, I'm Johnson. My secretary must have booked my ticket in my married name."

A low-level growl came from the other side of the counter.

All you can do is walk away. Today, the airline personnel have too much power. My husband is convinced that I'm going to be arrested for being belligerent to some $9.95 per hour employee who's going to make sure the friendly skies are safe from terrorist attacks. Right.

I turned and walked to one of the new self-check-in kiosks where you get five hundred bonus miles and don't have to deal directly with the PMS bitch. I bumped into a harried business traveler who was either Johnson or was under the same erroneous belief that the flight was wide open.

"Are you Johnson?"

He gave me a quizzical look.

"Because if you aren't Johnson, you aren't going to Vegas."

He ignored me and leaned over the counter and spoke in an almost whisper with the PMS goat. Then he turned around and muttered, "Shit."

I couldn't resist and smirked, "Told you. Come on, I'm heading to the United Club where sometimes I get untied. Yeah, I also know there are seats on that plane." Okay, I didn't say the bit about getting untied.

A beer in the United Club with an attractive companion, and life instantly improved. Time to go. Oops, gotta fill my pocket up with snacks and cheese and crackers so I can piss off whoever is sitting beside me when I have food to munch on and he or she is starving since the airlines can no longer afford to give out the puny snack bag with seven pretzels. God, I love to fly.

I do remember when it was fun. Guess it was about twenty years ago when five of us regularly traveled from Washington, DC, to Bakersfield, California, to work in the oil patch. No, not on a rig, just doing project reviews to make sure there were sufficient oil reserves in case those assholes in the Middle East decided to do another one of those oil embargos like in the early seventies.

Remember gas lines? What an easy pick-up place. The process was easy and better than a bar. I got several dates that way. Just pull in line behind a sports car, and after a while, everyone was outside the car bitchin' about what a pain in the ass the oil crisis is and how we should nuke the OPEC countries. Then you accidentally drop your open purse on the ground and kick your mascara under the hunk's car and give the guy a crotch shot as you gather your belongings. You were set for the night. Guaranteed.

Anyway, those were the good old days, traveling to Bakersfield. I even received the coveted "Down Hole Award" for my lewd activities in the oil patch. As I started to say, there were five of us who made this painful pilgrimage from Dulles once a month. The flight attendants loved us. We provided so much entertainment on the plane that no one watched the movie or grumbled about the mixed vegetables served with cold chicken breast or lack of pillows or the body odor of the four-hundred-pound person scrunched in the middle seat beside them or that the imported beer was Bud.

Those were the days when membership was ramping up in the Mile High Club. My charter membership card is still in my old jewelry box along with other date memorabilia—theater tickets, dead roses, hotel key cards, ticket stubs from Orioles World Series games, and semen-soiled memorabilia. Just kidding about the semen-tainted items. I did not kiss and tell or resort to blackmail.

Every trip, we came up with a reason why this trip was a major life event. John was going under cover in the oil field for four months to catch the perp that was working with the Japs and putting chemicals in the oil supply that would clog up the transmission on American gas-guzzling cars; Jim was missing the birth of his son; Dave got married the day before and was missing his honeymoon. You name it, we came up with the line and were routinely rewarded with a bottle of champagne. One time, Hertz decided that we had too much fun on the plane and wouldn't rent us a car until we sobered up. Had to walk across the street to a bar and have a couple beers until the Cordon Negro wore off.

Bakersfield.

That was the trip of all trips. Dave (the self-righteous program manager who was married to the Baptist minister's daughter who didn't own a tube of mascara or lipstick) and Colleen (the attorney who was living with a gay guy as a cover) were sleeping together. John held firmly to the theory of PCOT. That was Pussy-Cut-Off-Time, or six hours before flight time. He had some sexual inhibition about having sex with his wife less than twelve hours after he got out of bed with his final conquest from our favorite after-work country Western bar, the Funny Farm. Good rule. PCOT became the standard.

I had Greg, the FBI investigator who hung around the site trying to figure out what in the hell was really going on in the oil patch. He lived in San Francisco but could usually make the trip when the gang came to town. When we got home, we were so exhausted that our spouses felt sorry for the effort we spent in support of the nation's dwindling oil supply. We were family heroes.

Greg. He was one piece of meat. Until I found the oil patch, my sex life sucked. My husband was asocial, lot of money, cheap, had lots of Nazi memorabilia stashed in the closet, and hated people. He spent most evenings in his study communicating with green men from Mars. The Bakersfield gang decided that he was sent to Earth from Mars to figure out what was going on down here, and that was why he just didn't fit in. Not that he tried. Kinda like that show *My Favorite Martian* that we watched as kids. So Greg filled a justifiable need. My husband didn't even miss me. Even if he knew what was up, he just wrote it in his monthly progress report he transmitted to the green people. He thought it was what all Earthlings did. Guess the word "monogamy" is not in the Mars Berlitz study guide for non-English speaking green people.

At first the trips were all work and no fun. Then one night, we were sitting around the pool drinking beer, getting intoxicated from the sweet aroma of the night jasmine, and moaning about how hard life was, and we had an epiphany. We saw Dave and Colleen sneak around the corner into her hotel room—little too chummy for government work. We slithered across the pool area, led by a former Vietnam infantry captain, and listened for an hour to the moans emanating from behind the closed patio doors. Thank God they did not open the curtains. That event moved our mission at the patch in a new direction. If the boss was going to have such a good time out there, what about us?

Then John found this little filly at the Funny Farm, and PCOT was invented. That night, I had to be carried from the dance floor to the car to my room by Greg. I had twisted my ankle doing the Texas two-step because Fred put swizzle sticks and paper plates in my buttermilk, full-quill ostrich cowboy boots, which after too many beers on a previous trip I had picked up for the bargain price of $350 a foot. I guess the pre-Funny Farm cocktail hour impacted my cognitive abilities because I couldn't figure out why I couldn't get my feet in the boots correctly and did the most beautiful slip and fall to George Strait and "All my Exes Live in Texas."

We got back to room 210, and Greg carried me in and laid me on the bed. We just stared at each other. And stared at each other. I managed to pull myself up and stood beside him, leaning against the wall. Then we touched arms. In less than five seconds, clothes were strewn around the room. Hot passion. You read in novels how John runs his finger through Diane's mound of silky fur and finds his way into the deep damp moss. That's such bullshit. Sex was over in less than fifteen seconds, and we were in the prime of our sex lives. We were pre-Viagra. We looked at each other and laughed. It was the most unromantic, sexual experience that either of us had experienced at that time. Embarrassing. I had a man tell me that I did bad sex. I was a child from the sixties. I had a lot of experience. Sex was part of my being. So we began to practice, and I fell in love with a married man.

For the next two years, I had the most torrid love affair. We began to audit companies all across the county to determine their complicity in the oil crisis. We were feared in the industry. Tulsa, Houston, New Orleans. It was wonderful. I was the other woman. I was in lust. I even fell in love with country music because Conway Twitty could belt out songs that would make you hot just listening. When I would hear, "I Want a Man with a Slow Hand," that moss pit became a flowing river. Country music tells it like it is. The Funny Farm has amateur night every Thursday. One regular performer was a skinny roughneck who got up and crooned his newly penned song "Have a Cigar; Your Wife is Having My Baby." Help, gonna choke on my beer.

Those were the days when I was working on a new Hot List for *Cosmo*—sorry, *Condé Nast*—of hot of places to have sex. I thought it could go like this:

1. On the balcony of your hotel room with the opposing counsel the night following closing arguments in a contract dispute.

2. On the stairs with your boss outside his bedroom while his wife and your husband were sleeping off too many drinks after the dinner to celebrate your recent promotion.

3. Lying on the floor after the bed frame broke during your third orgasm of the evening.

4. Doing the Cabinet (having sex in the federal building for each cabinet agency). Getting the Department of State is the hardest of them all, so if you intend to try to accomplish this feat, focus there. Monica Lewinski was going for the Grand Slam— Executive, Judicial Senate, and House of Representatives—and she easily bagged the hardest one.

5. Hand sex at the top of the Ferris wheel at a Six Flags amusement park.

6. Under the boardwalk. (Thank you, Jay and the Americans).

7. In a car while your partner is driving.

8. Having sex anywhere in close vicinity to your partner's or your spouse if you're having an affair creates a high emotional ride.

9. Having sex where foreplay begins with you tied to the mast on a sailboat.

10. And, never forget the old standby:

11. Joining the Mile High Club on a 747.

Frances' wish list includes the Supreme Court. She doesn't give a rat's ass about doing a Grand Slam. I think that's because it took her five tries to pass the bar, and a Supreme Court fuck would be the most offensive means of retaliating against the American Bar Association for the agony she went through to join the elite ranks of sleazy barristers.

Sally CJ is thinking about the Library of Congress. Only a librarian would have the motto, "On my back in the stacks." Marcia wants to add the Louvre. Too bad I was there and didn't think of it!

Greg even brought his teenage kids to the beach when I went with my mother and a guy I was dating. Hugger-mugger. Look it up; it's the perfect descriptor of when sex is the best. It was like being back in high school and sneaking around the side of the house for a quick feel when your parents had your boyfriend over for a Sunday afternoon cookout after church.

Remember going steady in high school? Well, James Allen was my steady in tenth grade, but I couldn't admit that we were going steady because my parents didn't approve of the concept since I was too young to be tied down to one guy. My parents didn't approve of an intense monogamous relationship. When I heard them say, "Thank God Samantha Laraine and that boy with two first names have broken up," I usually had one waiting in the trenches ready to go. I loved to date guys with two first names, James Allen, Steven George, Ronnie Andrew, David John … just to piss them off.

Funny, when I was in high school, I thought monogamy was good and my parents insisted it was bad. During my first two marriages when I was in my twenties, monogamy was like a choker chain that was too tight around my neck. Maybe that's why I always had such an aversion to yanking our Samoyed's leash when he would lunge after a female dog. Then I'm in my twenties, and suddenly my parents do a 180 and insist that monogamy is good and tell me that I'm cursed by the devil since they suspect I have multiple sleeping partners, which, of course, I did.

Once you hit fifty, having a waiting list in the contact list on your iPhone is the way to go, according to Sally CJ, Frances, and Marcia. Fuck monogamy. By the way, Sally CJ thinks that PCOT is the dumbest thing she ever heard of. Fortunately, I'm finally at a point in life where I appreciate and honor the concept of monogamy. It just took me nearly forty years to understand the concept.

Anyway, back to Greg. I was getting ready to leave my third husband and made an offer on a house. Ready for monogamy, at last, so I thought. By that time, Greg's wife, a svelte little chick weighing in at 250, was fully aware of his infidelities and often used to accompany Greg on business trips. She would escort him to the office and sit outside like a sumo wrestler waiting. God, I loved it. What a challenge. That's when I learned conference room table sex. The thought of someone trying to open the door that had the chair propped under the doorknob like in the old Western movies was tantalizing. That was hot sex. At the end of the day, we'd walk to the door, and I'd wave to the fireplug waiting out front and go home to the Martian. I was just waiting for the result from the home inspection.

Life was good. Then one day, I was in a meeting, and my entire female staff came to the door and motioned me over. They couldn't be put off, so I excused myself. No, my parents weren't in a car accident. No, there was not a pink slip on my desk. My mind was racing. They said that I had a telephone call. They stood beside me and were prepared to provide comfort. I listened to what my friend who worked with

Greg was saying. Greg had died in his sleep. There would be no funeral. Family only. Being the other woman, I had no rights. There was no closure. How could this happen? Then a slight smile came across my face. Ann asked if I was okay. *Yeah,* I thought, *what a mess I would have been in if it had happened last week on the conference room table at Exxon corporate offices.* The next day, I met Steve. Life was good again.

Yes, we praise older women for a multitude of reasons. Unfortunately, it's not reciprocal. For every stunning, smart, well-coifed babe of fifty, there is a bald, paunchy relic in yellow pants making a fool of himself with some twenty-two-year-old waitress. I apologize.

—Andy Rooney

Don't Tell Me What to Do

To know us is to love us, or as many people sitting within twenty-five feet of us in an airplane or in a restaurant groan, to know us is to observe loud, obnoxious, middle-aged women who are pretty damned good looking and are obviously having an incredibly good time. How we wound up as buds though is a good question.

I'm a firm believer that the first day of your life sets the tone for years to come. My mother was a not so frail woman whose biceps were the size of the spinach cans that Popeye used to down when Brutus messed with Olive Oyl.

From what I've been told during familial reminiscing, I was over three weeks late, which was becoming a major inconvenience in my parents' social lives, so they scheduled to have labor induced. This appointment was a cause to celebrate, and after several bottles of MD 20-20, my future mother and father headed off to the delivery room. I guess Mom made such a good impression on the delivery room staff that she was shackled to the gurney in anticipation of the glorious event. Then there was a major car and bus collision on Thirty-Third

Street just down the street from the hospital, and all of the attending physicians rushed to the emergency room and left Maggie alone.

A shot of Pitocin coupled with high-end, good ole American wine and strapping tape left Popeye a pretty pissed off camper, who apparently needed a Lifesaver that was in her purse that was on a chair ten feet away. No one was around to hear her bellowing pleas, so she literally jumped the bed across the room while her limbs were firmly secured to it.

Then two hours later, and after an injection to knock her out and give the exhausted staff a break and peace and quiet, I slipped into the world. One banged up, shaken and stirred, little darling. A joy to behold. A *girl.*

Bad news. A girl was not on the agenda. Jonathan Edward Anderson IV was not to be born. And so my life began.

My son's birth was not quite so hostile. After twenty-eight hours of labor, my body was not working with me as forecast by Joyce Brown, and the doctor asked my son's father if he minded if they performed a C-section. Whose body was about to undergo the knife? Who had been demanding a C-section for the past three weeks? Who was becoming more agitated by the second? Who was becoming her mother?

Anyway, not long thereafter, they picked my then-husband off the floor and told him that he was the proud father of a son. Shit. Another penis in my life. After everyone was cleaned and sewed up, I was handed my twelve-pound little darling, who promptly shit all over me. What was that nonsense that they told you about a mother's unconditional love?

I guess I'm the fulcrum balancing the slightly opposing personality traits of Sally CJ, Frances, and Marcia. These traits were formulated during the same one-year window by totally different yet quite similar childhood experiences. After all, we were the girls of the sixties. Frances and I both are the older of two siblings, and both of us have a brother who's five years younger and not quite in touch with the world. We both married our high school sweethearts. Then, the similarity ends. Frances is a pleaser; I'm a renegade.

Sally CJ was part of a large Irish Catholic family and served as the matriarch. (Matriarch is defined as head bitch in charge of all siblings.) That would in all logic make her the matriarch of the group, the steadying and calming influence. Wrong. Sally CJ is the wild one—red hair, oppositional. "Don't tell me what to do!" is her favorite phrase. And there's no point in going against that dictum. Sally CJ cannot be told what to do.

You wonder why. What was it in her past that made her that way? At a time in her life when she should become accommodating, willing to conform to the group's best interest, all you get is don't tell me what to do.

I think it's because on the very first day of her life, she was sequentially defined. Her birth certificate looks like one of the first drafts of this novel. Scratch outs and pen and ink changes all over the place. First she was Mary Catherine. Then Mary Catherine, and she was Rebekka, then Rebekka, and she was Barbara Ann. What religion were her parents anyway? Catholic? Jewish? Presbyterian? Shit, no wonder the girl is such a mess today. She was also Sally for about thirty seconds. And finally the good old Irish Catholic influence won out, and she was back to Mary Catherine Justine McAllister or Sally CJ.

Sally CJ was the middle of seven children and lived on a big farm next to Lake Ontario in Upstate New York. Her older sister was blonde and petite with a peaches and cream complexion. Her younger sister was a raven-haired Irish beauty with milky skin, also petite and very witty. Both were the apples of their father's eye. Sally CJ was a clumsy, redheaded, freckle-faced tomboy, a "late bloomer" who constantly tripped up the stairs, spilled her milk, and spent most of her hours in the closet she shared with these two sisters reading a Victorian novel, praying she would become an only child, or at least develop breasts by the time she was out of high school so she would not be tormented by her sisters. They always called her a nerd and told her what to do and how to do it.

Well, the good fairy must have been living in the closet and took pity on the poor flat-chested redhead because much to the amazement of her sisters, not only did she develop breasts, but, at sixteen, 34DD breasts appeared on her tomboy body that made the red hair and freckles nonexistent in the minds of those testosterone-laden college boys who suddenly were not looking at the sisters but drooling at Sally CJ. Of course, at that time in her life, Sally CJ had no idea of the power of breasts, and she still preferred to read a good book as opposed to being subjected to the antics of teenage boys, but as the years wore on, Sally CJ soon learned how a great body coupled with a good brain could get you almost anything you wanted and used both as necessary. She learned she could go to Woodstock and still get a 4.0, or sit in the library until five and then go and drink and party until two in the morning and enjoy it all. This was the era of sex, drugs, and rock 'n' roll, remember.

Life was good.

Still somewhat of a nerd who still preferred books, Sally CJ went to grad school to be a librarian, wore halter tops while reading in the library, string bikinis with a book at the beach, and got a perverse thrill torturing men late into her twenties. When she finally got married (at the ripe old age of twenty-eight) it was because her husband to be was a schizoid personality just like she was—nerd party boy who got 800 on his math SATs but took six years to get out of college because he partied too much.

Just like in the romance novels, Sally CJ settled down into being the perfect wife and mother. She did all the right things—PTA, room mother, entertainer, cook, transportation coordinator, home laundry management, and other menial chores. She was told women could have it all. No one said that her life would be physically and mentally exhausting and leave her feeling empty and unfulfilled. Al took everything she did for granted. He was the typical macho guy who expected everything and gave nothing back.

We both lived in an affluent town where chauvinism was not only tolerated but encouraged. Women were not expected to work, men were the boss, and credit was in your husband's name, not your own. We were the outcasts. Professional women who loved to work but weren't keen about the other expectations in marriage.

That's when we met. We were living in the same town, our husbands worked together, both of us had ADD boys, and the only difference between us was I was still working and had a great fifth husband. The first words Sally CJ said to me clearly described where she was at in her personal struggles. "I didn't burn my bra in New York City to become a Stepford Wife," she growled when we were sitting outside the principal's office to discuss our sons' behavior issues.

She never said anything to anyone, but after twenty-five, years of a marriage where she was doing it all, she realized she didn't want the husband, or even the kids, but still wanted the romance of the affluent lifestyle. She divorced the husband, moved three hundred miles away to a small apartment, got a job as a librarian in a junior college, and told the kids she was going to do things her way from then on. No one was ever going to tell her what to do anymore. It's been that way ever since, and, man, is she having a good time. She probably has sex more than I do, at least it seems that way, and it's never "just sex." There's always a story that goes with it.

I can remember the first weekend she moved to Philadelphia. We were all worried and wanted to comfort her.

"No, thank you," Sally said over the phone. I could tell there was a huge grin on her face as she spoke. "Jim Roberts, a.k.a. Mr. Tucson, is coming to town to try out the New Zealand lambskin rug I bought for in front of the fireplace."

Never one to move slowly, Sally CJ had the guy she'd been scouting for years come up to spend the night with her the day after she moved into her new abode. This is the story she tells all divorcees who are reentering the dating game.

When Mr. Tucson first arrived, things were a little tense. However, after a couple glasses of Grey Goose and a candlelight dinner with a bottle of Chateau Leoville Las Cases 2005, fillets and garlic mashed potatoes, they were primed. Who needs a green vegetable anyway, and asparagus is always problematic. According to Sally, they had "mind boggling" candlelight sex, which started out on the new rug to the tunes of Van Morrison and finished up in her new bed with the 600-count sheets she had purchased from Neiman Marcus and had sent by overnight delivery the day before she arranged the date. Even though they cost a bazillion dollars, Sally CJ claimed they were clearly worth every penny—no rug or sheet burn on her fair ass.

As she tells the story, she and Mr. Tucson were lying there, exhausted, when Mr. Tucson says he's not feeling well, gets out of bed buck naked, and keels over (all 225 pounds of him). He hit his head on the nightstand, and blood was free-flowing everywhere. The white sheets were splattered with red dots. Sally CJ couldn't find the light switch to see if he was still alive, and she had this tremendous urge to wash the bed linens before the blood dried into a permanent pattern.

This was not a hotel. Sally CJ couldn't just grab her clothes and hope that he could sleep it off and call her in the morning. The scene gave her favorite phrase, "Fuck me," a new meaning. There was a potential stiff in her new house. A married-to-someone-else she fortunately did not know, potential stiff. She didn't even have time to wonder what the neighbors were going to think.

Sally CJ decided to call 911 but couldn't find the phone, much less remember the new phone number, the address, or even the closest cross road. All she knew was that she had to get him dressed and down the stairs before the paramedics arrived. This in itself was no small feat.

When the paramedics finally arrived, Sally CJ didn't know whether to tell them he was just there for the night as her lover, or make up some proper story about how they were having dinner as loving husband and wife, and he collapsed into the table by the fireplace.

She followed the ambulance to the hospital, and while the paramedics wheeled him to the ER, she was faced with the task of registering with the admission office. That, of course, required important data, such as insurance coverage, home address, and social security number. This necessitated either rifling through his wallet or contacting his wife.

She took the high road. "We were just married two weeks ago, and I'm not sure about his insurance coverage. Let me check." And she rapidly pulled out important documents from his wallet.

"We're in the process of moving here. Steve," cough, "I mean Jim, will be living in Tucson until the house sells."

Sally smiled, forged his name on the admitting forms, and tried to figure out how she was going to get the blood out of the sheets and carpet.

A couple hours later, the doctor came out of the ER and walked up to her. "Mrs. Roberts, your husband will be just fine. It appears he had a slight anxiety attack and passed out. The EKGs all came out just fine. It wasn't a heart attack."

Sally smiled. *Not only can I cook, I'm still good in bed*, she thought to herself.

"You can go back and see him. We gave him a slight sedative when we sewed him up, so he might be a little groggy."

Sally CJ grabbed his belongings and went back to room 5 as directed. She really wanted to go back to her house and clean up, but that wasn't what a loving wife would do in the situation.

A couple hours later, the nice nun who handled the admission brought the discharge papers. She handed them to Sally and told her to have his family doctor take out his stitches in about ten days. She gave Sally CJ that look like, "I know you're not his wife." At this point, Sally didn't care. She hailed Mr. Tucson a cab outside the hospital and sent him to the airport and went off to her new job.

As she said, Sally CJ is not taking any more shit from anyone. Amazingly, she and Mr. Tucson still get together every couple of months, and it's never happened again, but Sally CJ is sure it was the great sex that kept him alive, and she still proudly shows off the rug burns on her derriere.

Maybe that puts things in perspective. Sally CJ married Al later in life, at the ripe old age of twenty-eight. Shit. I had already been struggling with all that monogamy stuff for four years by then.

Marcia is another story.

> *I refuse to consign the whole male sex to the nursery.*
> *I insist on believing that some men are my equal.*
>
> *—Brigid Brophy*

½ Brain + ½ Body = 1 White Knight

I'm really lucky to have two great sisters-in-law. My brother's wife is a lot of fun, and it still amazes me that anyone that cool could remain married to my brother for over thirty years. Hell, Marie is ten years younger than I am, and all my marriages totaled together barely tally twenty years. That sounds like the beginning of one of those algebra problems you felt was so meaningless back in eighth grade. Use the formula and solve for "x." If Marie is ten years younger than Jane and has been married for five years longer than Jane, who has had four trips to the altar, plus a marriage at the Elvis drive-thru in Las Vegas, how many more times has Jane had oral sex than Marie?

It all goes back to that monogamy issue. Marie's mother left a trail of men in the past, so I think Marie sought out stability, and in my brother, that's what she got, stability, like a rock—no, more like the kind of knives they now give you in airplanes, dull but perfectly functional.

My brother and I were five years apart in age and really didn't know each other. He was the blessed savior. A boy, the continuation of the good old family name. One thing I always knew about Jonathan was that there would be no Johnny the Fifth on the family tree. Good boy. I know all siblings fight, but this child really pissed me off. I can still remember one Easter weekend when my parents felt it was safe to go across the street and play bridge and let me babysit my dear seven-year-old brother. Feeling religious, I decided that we could act out the Easter story, and since Jesus was a male, Jonathan was assigned the leading role. He probably should have been awarded an Oscar for his convincing portrayal of Jesus when I was stapling him to the basement door. Maggie heard the yelps from across the street and rescued him just in time. What was his bitch? I never got to be the star in a play.

Anyway, back to my other sister-in-law and the remaining member of the disaster team, Marcia, my husband's sister. I didn't meet her until the day of Graham's and my wedding reception. When she walked in the room, I couldn't believe the sight; there was my husband in a Dolly Parton wig. Talk about looking alike, incredible. The moment I met her, I knew why God made me finally decide to speak to Graham after intensely disliking him professionally for over six years. We were meant to be together. Not Graham and I, Marcia and I. I'm not sure she felt the same way initially, but she soon learned that her big brother had finally met his match.

Marcia is cute, bubbly, and manages to accomplish whatever task is to be done quietly and efficiently. That's the problem; she doesn't rock the boat enough to draw the attention of the proper male suitors. While Sally CJ and I often attract too much attention, Marcia is more restrained; she's an artiste. Unlike Frances, who's usually humiliated by our antics, Marcia provides encouragement to fuel the fire. She serves as the set-up queen.

She's the epitome of the perfect homeroom mother, the one who bakes the chocolate chip cookies that are so scrumptious they could be sold at Neiman Marcus. Perfect life. Right? Wrong. Marcia is a widow who has the ability to attract gorgeous guys with major character flaws, no money, and no job. Men who consider going to Home Depot to buy dry wall or going mud wrestling constitute a big night out. She seems to snare men that cannot afford to buy her a pony ride at the county fair. Oh, where is the knight in shining armor who's supposed to ride up on the white horse to sweep her off her feet? Yep, you got it … she's searching for a clone of her brother. At least she's not a death threat.

Marcia just ended a relationship with Pete, who was a great guy. He used to live in Chicago and was a senior partner in a law firm. Then one day he woke up and decided that what he really wanted to do was to live on a sailboat in South Carolina. It wasn't important that he had never been on a boat in his life. He said adios to his wife of forty years, gave her everything in the house and the Beemer, cashed out his law firm partnership interests, took the dog and headed south, let his hair grow into a ponytail, and bought a sailboat. Our major objective is to find the date to take us from rags to riches. As it turned out, Pete was Marcia's fifth rag in a row.

I really liked Pete, but it didn't take long to figure out that he wasn't a keeper. He was charming, educated, knew more about wine than I ever dreamed of, and once owned part of a racehorse. Probably even had a big dick. What more could a girl want? This was the first time that Marcia thought she hit the big one. She met Pete at a bar in some Podunk beach town while on holiday. Cool, debonair, sailboat, slicked back hair like Steven Segal, good teeth, had all the right moves, and a Visa with a $500 credit limit. Well, Marcia wanted that princess tiara, and she wasn't going to get it with Pete. Too bad. Gone but not forgotten.

Marcia's plight reminds me of an e-mail I recently received from a friend whose husband dumped her for a divorcee with three kids under ten.

From: Sue Jones
Sent: Saturday, December 01, 2011 11:03 a.m.
To: L.S.Anderson@aol.com
Subject: Who Can Understand Men?

Who can understand men?

1. *The nice men are ugly.*

2. *The handsome men are not nice.*

3. *The handsome and nice men are gay.*

4. *The handsome, nice, and heterosexual men are married.*

5. *The men who are not so handsome, but are nice men, have no money.*

6. *The men who are not so handsome but are nice men with money think we're only after their money.*

7. *The handsome men without money are after our money.*

8. *The handsome men who are not so nice and somewhat heterosexual don't think we're beautiful enough.*

9. *The men who think we're beautiful, that are heterosexual, somewhat nice, and have money are cowards.*

10. *The men who are somewhat handsome, somewhat nice, and have some money, and thank God are heterosexual are shy and* **never make the first move!**

11. *The men who never make the first move automatically lose interest in us when we take the initiative.*

Now ... who in the hell understands men?

Men are like a fine wine. They all start out like grapes, and it's a woman's job to stomp on them and keep them in the dark until they mature into something you'd like to have dinner with.

Send this to smart women who need a laugh and to the guys you think can handle it!

Done.

Well, Marcia responded to the e-mail within minutes of my hitting the enter key.

Now I'm worried, in fact, not just worried, I'm ready to call a tribal counsel and have the Bitch, Lush, and Slut descend upon the Princess Wannabe. I'm actually hyperventilating and need to take a couple Tagaments. Marcia has lost it. I think the experience with Pete did her in.

She's seeing an old friend from high school—a pediatrician, recently widowed, grown children, good teeth, full head of hair, and a platinum American Express card. He's been flying down to see her in his private jet for a couple weekends a month. She was moaning that she's exhausted. Amen! I told her she could retire all the battery operated toys, referred to as rabbits by one of my buds, and she said, "Oh, no, we don't live together."

I asked her what that had to do with not needing the rabbits, and she said, "I mean we're not in a sexual relationship."

The girl needs help.

Because we truly love her, we needed to postpone our scheduled reunion with the Mexican boys and help out one of our own. Besides, Marcia lives in Hilton Head, and any town that's named after a sexual act is good for the girls. So good-bye, Mexico. Hello, South Carolina.

Frances called me to bail out at the last minute because her boss thought that negotiating a major land acquisition in Poland was more important. There are times that I wonder if Frances really has her priorities in the right order. She doesn't speak Polish. The Poles don't have porcelain white teeth. In fact, I think it's considered good if Poles have 75 percent of the basic set. To make her recusal even more unusual, she was flying in coach class with her boss who was single and at least fifty pounds overweight.

My phone rang, and I glanced at the caller ID and saw it was Sally CJ. "What is this about Frances and Poland?" I demanded.

"Don't you mean Prague?"

"She said she told you. She can't come to Hilton Head because she's going to negotiate a contract in Poland."

"Are you sure she said didn't say Prague?" I was beginning to smell a rat.

"It's definitely Prague. We even joked about a recent article in a travel magazine that claimed Prague's the hottest ticket in Eastern

Europe for a romantic getaway—and how romantic is that tub of lard boss of hers?"

"What are you talking about? Romance in Prague? What about work in Poland?"

"See what happens when you become an old, married fuddy-duddy? You're out of touch with what's in. For your information, Prague has undergone profound changes in the past few years. The city is glitzy and routinely visited by film stars and artists. There's great music, exquisite castles, museums, churches, garnets, crystal, delicious gourmet cuisine, inexpensive prices, unsurpassed charm, fun—"

"Okay. Stop right there. Movie stars, artists, crystal. What is she up to?" From our many Friday night game sessions, I know that Frances is not geographically challenged, so the fact that she interchanged Prague and Poland means she's up to something. "

"I don't, know but maybe she's getting lucky and doesn't want a bunch of shit from us."

"Well, we can deal with that snake later. We need to find out why Marcia is becoming a nun."

Marcia was thrilled that we were coming and planned a small party to introduce us to the Hilton Head crowd. Besides, with the help of her newly found resources, she had added a swimming pool and hot tub to her backyard, and we would be there to celebrate the grand opening.

The intimate party turned into quite a bash. It seems that Marcia's beau went to college with Joe Walsh, who was known back then as the "phantom of Kent State," and we were entertained after dinner by the Eagles. You got it … "Get Over It!" in person. I'd go to the Hotel California with those guys anytime. Marcia's life had definitely taken a turn for the better. Why no sex? She had never saved herself for anyone in the past. Why was Steve not being more aggressive? The ugly potential of his sexual preference was hanging over the party like a major thunderhead. The good thing was that everyone else, including Marcia, was wearing blinders.

Was the opportunity to party with the likes of the Eagles worth a permanent relationship with Mr. Rabbit? That is a tough one, but I'll take the real thing.

Meanwhile, Sally CJ was christening the hot tub in search of the real thing. There were ten people in the hot tub, and for some reason Sally CJ was focusing her attention on this balding guy that reminded me of Mr. Peabody from the *Rocky and Bullwinkle Show*.

I noticed that Mr. Peabody was with a date that could have been a model for *Vogue*. What did this guy have to get a date that could have been a twin sister of Elle or one of the Hilton sisters, and have Sally CJ hot on the prowl? It definitely had to be more than a good personality.

"Hey, girl, what am I missing? What is it with Mr. Peabody?" I commented as I handled Sally CJ a fresh margarita.

"Look at the size of those hands."

"Yeah. So?"

"Where have you been? Haven't you read the recent studies that report that penis size is directly proportional to hand size? And, my sweet, that guy could palm a watermelon."

And with that pronouncement, Sally CJ continued her game of underwater pecker peaking in the direction of Mr. Peabody.

After an hour of mingling with the guests, my jetlag caught up, so I left Sally CJ happily playing underwater pecker hide and seek and headed to bed, where I tried to figure out what was wrong. That was when I realized Marcia was using the wrong formula to search for the perfect mate. I had made this mistake in selecting my second husband when I was searching for a rich spouse because I was tired of running out of money the last week of the month and living off of popcorn and oranges.

My flawed search criteria were:

Objective: Rich spouse who liked to travel

Criterion One: At least ten years older and intelligent

Criterion Two: Minimal debt

Criterion Three:	Owned house over 3,500 square feet
Criterion Four:	Drove sporty car
Criterion Five:	Older parents with considerable wealth
Criterion Six:	No previous wife with alimony or child support obligations
Criterion Seven:	No siblings
Criterion Eight:	Enjoyed travel
Criterion Nine:	Employed in a high-wage earning position
Criterion Ten:	Physically attractive, within proper weight limits

Looked like it should work. The successful candidate had to meet all ten criteria. I went through several candidates and, during the dating process, managed to eat at the top twenty-five restaurants recommended by the *Washington Post* and *Washingtonian* magazine.

While we were dating, Doug and I went to Hawaii, France, and the Caribbean. It would be a perfect marriage. I received a two-carat flawless diamond for an engagement offering along with a prenuptial agreement for my execution. Note, I did not say gift. Gift means not to be returned. The girls were outraged that I would consider signing a prenup, but why not? I was going to be rich. Where else was all that money going to flow when my husband died? Anyway, I would have a great time before that happened!

We married, a year later Alex was borne, and the next thing I knew, the Corvette was replaced by a Ford Taurus. Then there were notes on my desk stressing the benefits of breastfeeding and the benefit of stay-at-home moms.

Trouble was looming.

The second Christmas, I received a new doorknob for the front door. I knew Christmas was going to be lean on the gift side when Doug brought home a fresh cut Christmas tree that I suspected came from the neighbor's side yard.

The next birthday, I gave myself a new house and left.

The flaw in my criteria—I did not include "likes to spend money." That dude will probably line his coffin with dollar bills and give the rest to the PETA or some other important organization.

I realized as I lay in my Duxana bed, with the mattress design based on technology from NASA, that Marcia had a flawed checklist:

I think hers was ½ hunk + ½ party guy = 1 white knight.

That would never work. As I rolled over to go to sleep, I knew that Sally and I had our work cut out for us over the next few days.

What went wrong? Again, I think back on her childhood and what did her in. Aha, I remember the big family reunion Graham and I had our first Christmas after we were married. The reunion that included his stepbrother, Steven, and Steven's pregnant German wife who did not speak English and their three kids under the age of four, Marcia and her fourteen-year-old son, Graham's thirty-five-year-old son and the girlfriend he was ready to break up with, my hyperactive eight-year-old, the dog, the bird, the hamsters that the teenage salesgirl at the pet store assured me were both males and their recent litter of six, and Frances sans date, all who were living under the roof of my house.

In looking at the pictures and home movies, it's obvious how we survived. We drank. The picture of me mooning Graham and Marcia after Christmas Eve dinner is particularly memorable. I know Graham wasn't blushing; it was a semipermanent glow from the single malt Scotch.

Anyway, in the middle of Christmas dinner, Marcia rose from her chair and silenced everyone to make a major pronouncement. We immediately assumed there was a new suitor who was about to arrive. Oh, did I mention that Marcia is Graham's half-sister? Graham's mother moved to the States with an American GI shortly after WWII, and Graham stayed in Scotland with his father.

He didn't visit his mother until his father passed away and he decided he needed to get some good old American culture. He had never heard or baseball and didn't even know what blue jeans were when he arrived in Youngstown, Ohio. And he thought rubbers were used to erase mistakes, not prevent them. Anyway, when he joined his mother, Marcia was a year old, and he was a teenager. She always admired her half-brother. He was her hero.

Marcia had commanded the attention of the group. We waited to hear about the new love of her life and how we were going to have to behave when he waltzed in the house momentarily. We were wrong. The news was that Graham was not her half-brother, or conversely, Steve was not her biological brother.

See, Marcia was separated at birth from her true kin and is still searching for him in her pursuit of happiness and the fucking white horse. She just needs to get the search criteria correct.

Belladonna /n/ in Italian, beautiful lady; in English, a deadly poison. A striking example of the essential similarity of the two languages.

—Ambrose Bierce

In Search of the Big Salami

We are all in search of the Big Salami.

Even those of us who are comfortably attached still cannot help but gaze at restricted areas and drool at off-limit potential.

We just got back from another year in Bermuda. I'm still alive and well, Sally CJ is unbelievably horny, and long-time very conservative friends that we invited down for a couple of days are still in shock.

Things were dull in Bermuda. There were no unattached men anywhere on the eastern side of the island. We're not addressing Frances's preferences, such as teeth, hair, money, employment, an ability to speak in sentences, an ability to answer at least one question in the Sunday *New York Times* crossword puzzle … I mean *no men, period.*

Friends from the DC area decided to join us for a few days. Sally CJ was stressed that this could impact her trolling activities. What if she couldn't sleep and went for a walk at two in the morning, and George Clooney was sitting on a bench staring at the moon because he was also having a bout with insomnia? She knew Michael Douglas had a house on the island. What if he sleepwalks? How could she be expected to bring him back to the cottage for a romantic interlude? Our bedroom was upstairs, and after we passed out at night, Sally CJ had the entire first floor living area to serve as the bachelorette pad. Now with Jim and Jill sleeping on the living room couch, she was going to have to drag either Mr. Clooney or Mr. Douglas into her room without any preparatory couch time.

I knew that this meant bad things were in store for Jim and Jill. The smile Sally CJ gave them as they dragged three suitcases, two sets of golf clubs, and scuba gear into the twelve-by-fifteen-foot living room was a dead giveaway. "Hi, guys, I am sooo glad you could join us here this week," she said with the warmth of a New Yorker, and, "When do you leave again?" a barely audible mutter under her breath.

Well the lack of men helped Sally CJ accept the fact that the likelihood of getting laid was pretty slim, so we decided to have a party. And, let's say Sally CJ really knows how to throw a party. She had to take the edge off, so one night she decided to give lap-dancing lessons. I suspect in Bermuda that could result in twenty to life in prison.

If you can picture trying to teach a mannequin how to lap dance, that's where we started. Jim and Jill were a little stiff. "More liquor," chanted Sally CJ. "Make it a double Dark and Stormy, pool boy," i.e., my poor husband.

Even though I now live in Las Vegas, I wasn't familiar with lap dancing. Wow. Now I have a much better appreciation of what goes on at the Olympic Garden (OG as the natives call it). When Frances comes to town, I know she goes there with a couple of women from her office. She's never been willing to go into any details about what they do there, and now I understand why. I think she's embarrassed about having an orgasm just because some nearly naked guy is massaging her lap with a large sausage, or shall we call it the Big Salami?

What makes us so different? I know our upbringing plays a large role in shaping our views, but maybe it goes further back in time to the day of conception. Let's see.

Sally CJ was born on November 10. That would make her approximate conception date on Valentine's Day. What are you thinking about on Valentine's Day? That's right, men, sex, sex, and more sex. That's definitely Sally CJ.

Frances's birthday is May 11, and Marcia was born a few days earlier. Obviously their parents were drinking at the beach. Good bodies, big smiles, spending money on vacation. Makes sense. The three main search criteria for both of them.

My birthday, on the other hand, is August 1. That would mean my parents were doing the dirty deed after Thanksgiving dinner. I like birds and have a pet parrot named Eddie who has the vocabulary of a steel mill worker. I also flatuate at an ungodly rate after eating stuffing and sauerkraut. Great.

It's obvious that the date of conception plays a huge role in genetics.

I e-mailed photos of the Bermuda trip to Sally CJ and Jill. Pictures of Sally CJ sandwich dancing with Graham and Jim, Jill passed out from the stress of her first lap-dancing session, Sally CJ and I posing with pina coladas by the pool, Sally CJ crammed into my two-piece bathing suit (don't get jealous, Pamela Anderson), Graham checking out whether Sally CJ's 34DDs are really larger than my 34Cs, and many more. I hope Sally's e-mail isn't screened by the college where she's an assistant dean. They think she's prim and proper.

Sally CJ responded with a short note that thanked me for the pics and stated that she was giving up on men because she was sick of the dating game. What went wrong?

I remember the time when getting a date was not the problem. The problem was how to juggle a number of guys so they had no clue there was competition. I had a problem of charming men at the negotiating table, having a celebratory drink in the local hotel bar, and then solidifying the relationship afterward in the sack. Through this process, I began to establish a dating source in a variety of cities. The intent was that I would come to them; they were not supposed to come to DC. I will never forget the time George from Seattle called from National Airport to surprise me and arrange a meeting at the Hyatt on Capitol Hill.

That same time, Greg was in town to plan an audit of books of a crooked oil company and conduct an in-depth review of my pubic hairs. Greg always stayed at the Capital Hyatt. I knew there was great potential that I would be more than fucked! Somehow I managed to have lunch and dessert with George on the fifth floor and dinner and Courvoisier with Greg on the seventh floor. I was stressed for days. Today I would be worrying about the calories from the liquor and drawn butter with the lobster. Back then I was worried about losing a potential date. Little did I appreciate what a good thing I had going. When you hit fifty, you don't get a date without considerable effort.

The search for the Big Salami is hard work and I now believe is for the young. It takes a lot of stamina and requires no shame. When you consider dating multiple men on work-related projects, remember there's always the possibility that they could meet, so the basic rulebook states: never sleep with more than one man who works with you at a time. Violations of this basic principle can be deadly.

If Sally CJ is giving up dating, that can only mean one thing. I think she's planning to harm me. Her message included the following attachment.

The Man Test

1. In the company of females, intercourse should be referred to as:
    a. Lovemaking
    b. Screwing
    c. Taking the pigskin bus to tuna town

2. You should make love to a woman for the first time only after you both have shared:
    a. Your views about what you expect from a sexual relationship
    b. Your blood test results
    c. Five tequila slammers

3. You time your orgasm so that:
    a. Your partner climaxes first
    b. You both climax simultaneously
    c. You don't miss ESPN Sports Center

4. Passionate, spontaneous sex on the kitchen floor is:
    a. Healthy, creative love-play
    b. Not the sort of thing your wife/girlfriend would agree to
    c. Not the sort of thing your wife/girlfriend needs to ever find out about

5. Spending the whole night cuddling a woman you've just had sex with is:
    a. The best part of the experience
    b. The second best part of the experience
    c. $100 extra

6. Your wife/girlfriend says she gained five pounds in the last month. You tell her that it is:

    a. Of no influence on your affectionate feelings toward her
    b. Not a problem, she can join your gym
    c. A conservative estimate

7. You think today's sensitive, caring man is:

    a. A myth
    b. An oxymoron
    c. A moron

8. Foreplay is to sex as:

    a. An apetizer is to an entrée
    b. Primer is to paint
    c. A long line is to an amusement park ride

9. Which of the following are you most likely to find yourself saying at the end of a relationship?

    a. "I hope we can still be friends."
    b. "I'm not in right now, please leave a message at the beep."
    c. "Welcome to Dumpsville. Population You."

Maybe we were in need of an intervention. I definitely needed to distract Sally CJ.

When we moved to Las Vegas, Graham was worried that I would have trouble adjusting. How do you take a Washington, DC, lawyer from the tight-ass corporate world to an environment void of pinstripe suits, white blouses, Hermes scarves, two-inch pumps, nude nail polish and clients? A place without an ocean where the sharks would never attack an attorney out of professional courtesy to the desert where sharks showed no favoritism in collecting gambling debts. Yes, Graham was worried about how to protect our retirement savings from the craps and blackjack tables and most of all, the sports book.

So during one of his early pre-relocation business trips to Vegas, he learned there was a senior women's softball team in town. I had played ball most of my life and was on a team in Northern Virginia that I was going to miss more than K Street.

My first week in town, I received a call from a woman asking if I would like to join the local softball team. They were just forming and had the aspiration of becoming national senior women's champions. I didn't tell them that there was no shot in hell of beating my Virginia girls but went to practice out of curiousity and impending boredom.

That's where I met Linda and Pansy. No kidding. Her real name on her birth certificate is Pansy Jo Jamison. Both were retired and were nothing like the women I had played ball with back east. Linda was a former cop in Chicago who had jet-black hair that was pulled straight back in a ponytail, and I was instantly afraid of her. Pansy Jo, who also had several inches on me, was previously in "the business" in Las Vegas and had recently started a new venture that was becoming a huge success.

After the first practice and initial introductions, we went to Dugan's for a beer and to get better acquuainted. I was a bit uncomfortable that practices started at 9:00 p.m. due to the heat, and our after practice get together started around midnight. Back east, you're already in a deep sleep at that hour.

"So, Pansy, tell me about your new business. I'm a commercial transactions attorney and can help you if you need any contract documents reviewed. I'm not sure what I'll be doing out here, so I have plenty of time available," I commented once the first round of Coors Lights were placed in front of us. I decided to go with the locals and not get a Guinness or Becks so they wouldn't think I was a snob.

"I host Pleasure Parties," Pansy said just as I took my first sip of beer.

After Pansy and Linda wiped the beer off their shirts that squirted out of my mouth as I choked, Pansy continued. "Yes. I host parties where I guide women in the fine art of pleasuring the penis."

So not only did Linda scare me because she was five feet ten and built like Rocky, Pansy scared me because I was so far out of my comfort zone. Both Linda and Pansy assured me that it was a completely legitimate business.

Pansy explained, "My goal is simple. Women don't like to give BJs because they're intimidated by penises. I take that fear away and help them learn how to make love to a penis. As a Pleasure Princess, I come to the party with training tools, which includes three suitcases containing multiple size and color penises. Each woman picks a penis, and I provide instruction on how to make your chosen penis your best friend. I teach the fine art of licking, sucking, carressing, massaging, and playing with your toy. You learn how to completely control your man." She said all of this as if she was pitching a potential acquisition in a corporate boardroom. Pansy definitely was not intimindated by a penis.

In the DC area, women host tupperware parties, jewelry parties, makeup parties, book parties, and children's birthday parties. I had been in Las Vegas for less than a week and felt like it could open doors to a completely new adventure.

Pansy might just be the cure for whatever's ailing Sally CJ. I think they just might give each other a run for the money. I know Sally CJ is an avid fan of controlling her man, and we all know a man's number-one brain is below the waist. So according to Pansy, control the penis, control the man.

Macho does not prove mucho.

—Zsa Zsa Gabor

The Utilitarian Fuck

I'm sitting in the conservatory at Frances's house waiting for her sorry ass to get home from a date weekend in DC. In cruder lingo, she had planned an exchange of bodily fluids resulting from an ongoing Internet encounter that was about to get physical.

Anyway, I'm exhausted from crawling through the bathroom window, which is always left open for Agatha the cat's ingress and egress. Even during the eight weeks Frances spent in Poland taking a summer course in Conflict of Laws and Business Economics, the window was open. Yeah, we all thought she was a little touched going to Poland to learn Business Economics, but logic is not a word that comes up very often when you describe Frances. I must admit though, when she came home, she did try to get all of her friends (?) to buy stock in a Polish telephone company that wound up taking the stock market crash even harder than Enron and all of the dotcom companies combined. I still wonder if there are telephones in Poland.

I never seem to remember to bring the key to Frances's house. I guess it's because I can always rely on the fact that the bathroom window will be open, rain or snow, -10 degrees or 100 degrees. Agatha has needs, you must understand. Yes, she has a litter box. I'm talking about the need to stalk the innocent birds and bunnies in Squirrel Hill and bring her trophy home to her proud mother. Some of us used to get off when our son won a motorcycle race or hit a home run with bases loaded in the ninth. Frances, being childless, has to get her jollies when Agatha has a successful hunt.

Frances and Adonis had a very ugly break-up. It turned out that his willingness to do special projects around her house was tied to his desire to move up the corporate ladder, as I suspected, and his close working relationship with Frances helped open a few doors on the executive floor, and before she knew it, the good old boys' club had some new blood, and he was hovering one rung above her. He was looking down on her, and it was not because they were in the missionary position. I think this one is called the "kiss my ass, I'm out of here, babe" position. Fortunately, Adonis, with his newly acquired title of vice president of business development, was transferred to Phoenix. Out of sight and out of mind. Yeah right.

I had warned her of the pitfalls of dating in the workplace if it wasn't for professional personal gain. Projects around the house do not qualify as for professional personal gain and can only lead to trouble. Whether we want to admit it or not, it's very difficult for a woman to maintain a purely sexual relationship without emotional involvement. We seem to have the need to say the L word and thus open up the door to emotional attachment.

When I was in my late twenties, I learned that sex in the workplace was a two-edged sword. As a young woman just out of college and a newly married for the first time child of the sixties, I started my first job at NASA as a naïve, perky blonde with hair the same length as my suit skirt. The first indication that it wouldn't be all work actually occurred during my job interview, which went something like this.

"Do you do drugs?"

"No, sir."

"Do you smoke pot?" Remember it was the late sixties.

"Oh my, no, sir."

"Well, do you at least drink?"

"Oh yes. I've been drinking beer since I learned to crawl. I used to slither around on the patio during my parents' pool parties and drain empty bottles of Natty Boh that were left unattended on the ground. Hated those cigarette butts in the empties, however." Well I actually omitted the part about the Natty Boh.

"You're hired. Go to personnel Monday morning. Welcome aboard."

My total vision of work was shattered during my first postlaunch party. Only three months earlier, I had pledged my heart and soul "until death do we part" to my high school sweetheart, with the blessing of his minister father, minister uncle, and the then church minister. I was literally triple married forever and ever, amen, or was each minister's blessing only good for a month?

Maybe in the real world the sanctity of marriage has a deep meaning, but that was not the case at NASA during the height of the space program. After 5:00 p.m., NASA had nothing to do with space. It really stood for "**N**aughty **A**nd **S**exually **A**ctive" postcollege professionals. Within days of being hired, I was introduced to the coed softball league. I played on a team called "XXX," and we played braless and had an ever-growing fan base. But the best company events were parties after launches, and shortly after my employment started, there was a launch party that took me over a decade to recover from. In fact, it took the untimely death of Mr. Warren to free me of the demon of that night. The Rec Center was packed, and the liquor was flowing like an erupting volcano—hot, hot, and really hot.

This was not like a typical frat party. Launch parties were testimony as to why you should never marry your high school sweetheart immediately after college. During those four long years of studying where you were programmed to make good grades so you could get the perfect job and make money to acquire meaningless material possessions, you had the safety net of the academic world and no idea what pursuing a career entailed.

After the honeymoon, you were in a happy, monogamous state, believing that Ozzie and Harriett were real people. It doesn't take long to discover that, notwithstanding the diamond on your left hand, your hormones are still in a raging state, and there are many wolves ready to pounce. A recent national opinion poll found that a person doesn't reach adulthood until the age of twenty-seven. That may seem old to a college graduate; however, back in the early seventies, I could provide documented proof that the age of maturation of the male sex is well into the late forties. Then a decade later at fifty, men enter midlife crisis, cheat on their wife, wreak havoc on the family, and settle in with the new babe sans children and other perceived family baggage.

As I surveyed the crowd, I felt a hand on my thigh and looked over my shoulder only to see the husband of one of my mother's best friends, and an attendee at my not too distant wedding reception.

"How's it going? Still playing golf?"

Shit. What could I say? "My mom always wanted to get in your pants?"

Was it up me to take one for the old neighborhood? No. Thank God I was saved by Connie, my fellow trainee and leader into areas you cannot enter with a conscience, and ultimately the godmother to my son many years later. Connie gracefully slid in between my mom's dream date and me, hooked her arm in his, and headed off toward the bar, gone for the evening. Connie was entering into a proper, professional dating workplace relationship and was soon on a fast-track to an SES level position.

So after recovering from the Adonis embarrassment, Frances decided to approach men with a two-prong attack. She entered law school and the world of Internet dating. She maintained that law school was for career advancement and provided a vast dating pool of men who, after graduation, passing the bar, and a few years at a prestigious law firm, could afford to finance her clothing budget.

Being a savvy business woman, she had a clearly defined screening process for candidates identified on match.com and eHarmony. I'm not exactly sure how she prequalified men, but I would imagine that she got the vital information utilizing courtroom skills learned in Moot Court by asking some very carefully disguised questions.

To check teeth, she would say:

"I had to change dentists because of my dental plan, and I had my initial appointment yesterday with a new dentist. I can't believe that she had the audacity to suggest that I need braces since my teeth are beginning to show stress fractures due to the purported fact (terminology only fitting since she's a budding esquiress) my bite is not perfect. I can't imagine what it would be like to have braces. Did you ever have to wear them when you were a child?"

To check hair:

"My best friend's husband is starting to lose his hair and is really obsessed with the fear of going bald. I told her that a lot of jocks have thinning hair on the top, like Cal Ripken, and that he'll eventually get over it. Do you have any advice? Maybe Rogaine will help. He's such a nice guy. I told her that I don't think balding is that big of a deal. Why are men so obsessed with a little thinning on the top?"

To check credit worthiness:

"Can you believe that one of the women in my office only has a $1,500 limit on her Visa card? She went to charge a sixty-inch flat screen and entertainment center, and the card wouldn't accept the charge. Amazing. I thought everyone has at least a $20,000 limit on their Visa."

To check potential of gut:

"God, I went to the gym yesterday, and every man had a gut so large he looked at least five months pregnant."

To check out ethnic heritage:

"Do you like mageritsa?" If he has any idea what you're talking about and replies in the affirmative, do not date. Greeks are trouble.

Anyway, I had to come to Pittsburgh earlier in the day because my hair was beginning to look like a floor mop, and Frank decided it was time for me so go back to my Diane Sawyer platinum blonde newscaster look. I hate it, but Frank is the "hair man" and is rarely too far off. Now it's Saturday evening, and I'm perched on a beautiful leather couch from Roche Bobois that Agatha uses to keep her claws primed for the hunt. I'm sipping ten-year-old vintage Bordeaux from a vineyard in Margaux out of a chipped Reidel wine glass, waiting for Frances to get home and fill me in on the law school date pool and the first real encounter with John. That's typical of all of our lives: good wine, chipped glass; good teeth, no hair; full head, no money; great body, full head, sexual problems.

I think she believed that the law school would offer a better selection of qualified men, but in the meantime, she had been having a torrid e-mail/texting/phone relationship with John for three months when they decided it was time to meet. Well, you can get all that vital data, have daily chatter bordering on erotica, and still not know the guy. After an exhausting week of classes at school, Frances and John finally met for dinner at L'Auberge Chez François in Great Falls, Virginia. I suspect that was part of the credit worthiness test and was surprised when she didn't push for the Inn at Little Washington. I guess that was a little too remote if the date was a dud. By staying local, if John was still a viable candidate after dessert, they could have a night cap at the townhouse she rented on Capitol Hill.

When she slammed front door and flopped down on the other end of the couch, I knew that something happened and there was a story forthcoming. And this is how the story unfolds. "John excused himself and went to the bathroom, so I darted into my bedroom to make the last-minute checks—no spinach between the teeth, little dash of Channel No. 5 in all the right places, check to make sure the ridged Trojans were in the night table, fluffed hair, rushed back into the living room. No John. Rushed back in the bedroom to grab another Trojan to hide in the couch in the living room just in case, uncorked a bottle of wine, and assumed a pose on the couch right out of Penthouse."

She waited. Ten minutes passed. Another ten minutes. *Fuck me*, she thought. *What if he's dead in the bathroom?* She immediately called Sally CJ since she's our expert on the subject of potential dead man in house. No answer.

After three unsuccessful tries, she claimed to have called me, but I didn't answer. I was probably napping after the exhaustion from climbing through the bathroom window. I reminded Frances that I'm not much good in this area. My only date-death experiences were the fantasy dreams of one of my former bosses and of course Greg who was considerate enough to die in bed with his wife after he got home.

After listening intently to the story, I said "So how was your date?"

"All I can say is that he fixed my plumbing," smiled Frances.

"Good, you needed that."

"I mean he worked on the toilet. And I got laid, so I guess you could call it a Utilitarian Fuck. We didn't exactly have a lot in common, and he might not want to see me again."

Okay, what's the first question that comes to your mind? "Did you have sex before or after he fixed the toilet?"

"Please."

"Okay. Was sex the reward for services rendered?"

"No way. He went to the bathroom to check for food in his teeth, comb his thinning hair, loosen his tie, and maybe to pop a little blue pill, and then he saw the replacement part for the toilet sitting on the sink. And voila! The rest is history. The toilet no longer leaks. It was not sex for payment for services. I didn't expect him to go into immediate handyman mode; I was laying groundwork to discuss the potential for a future service call. It's very hard to find a trustworthy handyman in DC, especially when I have to shuffle back and forth between DC and the Burgh."

Two birds (or plumbing needs) killed with one date.

Well, Frances has a lot more handyman activities scheduled, so I'm sure she isn't going to let this one get away. There are a lot of benefits associated with a Utilitarian Fuck.

Anyway, after Adonis and a few more Internet dating fiascos, Frances had sworn off men. The UF guy is still in the picture in DC, but I think she was honest in saying there was no romance. I don't think she's even home when most of the work is being done.

We finished the wine and a black Sambuca chaser and went to bed. In the morning, I got up early, tossed my gift from Agatha out the window into the garden, and ran up to 7-11 to get the paper. Frances had coffee and breakfast ready in the conservatory when I returned.

We were shoveling bagels slathered with lite cream cheese and mounded with globs of sugar-free strawberry jam in our mouths, reading the *Washington Post* and *New York Times*, and grazing through Sunday morning TV shows. Frances landed on a show about the ultimate weekend pastime—vehicle races. Not car races, vehicle races—school bus races, camper races, races with cars towing boats. It was a hoot. The school bus races took us back to our childhood. After clips of a race, a reporter was interviewing the driver of *Junkyard Dog*.

Frances quipped, "Now, I could do that!"

I agreed that racing busses would be a hoot.

"No," she replied. "I mean I could do him."

I guess the concept of a moratorium on sex without prequalifying standards is over. I hope short-term memory loss of giving up her prescreening process of men isn't an early sign of Alzheimer's.

Getting along with men isn't what's truly important. The vital knowledge is how to get along with a man. One man.

—*Phyllis McGinley*

A Misplaced Need of Fulfillment

My problem is that I'm happily married and beyond the dating game. Since the girls always seem to be in and out of relationships, are stressed about the aging process and wondering if any man can fall in love with flab and sag, I should be happy. I guess that's another problem for aging Type-A women; we just cannot be satisfied with the status quo. For the past year, I had been whining that I wanted to be a grandmother. I think it's one of the rites of passage with turning fifty. It is said when a women talks to her adult child about her biological "granny clock" ticking.

Those maternal longings were completely eviscerated after I volunteered to babysit on a Saturday night for a client I had recently irritated during litigation of a contract claim where we didn't come out on the winning side.

All I can say is that you forget what a child is like. You get into a grandma mode because of all the frilly dresses in the malls. Have you noticed that baby clothes are everywhere? They're not hidden in stores. There are "Granny, unlock your wallet" kiosks in the malls with the most adorable clothes you've ever seen. There's this subliminal message: "Give me a cute little granddaughter so I can dress her up."

Well, never mind. I arrived early for a kiddie refresher course before I was left alone with a six-year-old and three-year-old twins. Sherry was at least twenty months pregnant and wanted to have some quiet time with her husband, Darrell, before the next little darling joined the zoo. She got married for the first time at the ripe old age of thirty-nine and decided to immediately belt out babies.

Her first contribution to mankind was Darrell, an adorable little boy. He has to be adorable with the name Darrell. He's quite a precocious child and walks into a room, extends his hand, and introduces himself. "Hi. I'm Darrell, and here's my brother, Darrell, and my sister, Darla, and over there is my daddy, and he's a Darrell, too!" No, Sherry is not from West Virginia. She just made the mistake of marrying into a family with a deep psychological issue with naming offspring. Her husband, Darrell John Dupinski, who goes by Jack, is a really nice guy who inherited a bad family trait. All ten of the Dupinskis have "Darrell" as one of their given names. The younger Darrell is actually Edward Darrell and goes by Eddie. At the age of six, her oldest son already likes to manipulate facts and words and will probably become a politician.

 Need I say more, Sherry is still Sherry Franklin, and the child to be born is going to be Marjory Ellen. Not that great, but at least there are no Ds in either name.

Put your hands over your ears and close your eyes, remember those awful moments of motherhood, and get your old Patty Play Pal out of the attic. I'm withdrawing all requests for a grandchild because the term grandma means babysitting, i.e., a period of hours where you crawl on the floor making ridiculous car sounds, where your graduate school command of the English language turns into gibberish, where an evening curled up reading John Grisham or doing the *New York Times* crossword puzzle is a remote dream, and when you realize that the smell of poop cannot be tolerated for more than fifteen minutes without making you want to vomit.

I got so exhausted I gave the little angels a box of magic markers that I thought were washable, put on my running bra and shorts, and lay down on the kitchen floor and became a human coloring book. The kids were quiet for hours. Sherry and Darrell laughed the next day when I was moaning that I missed the word "permanent" on the markers. After all, what responsible parent would keep permanent magic markers in a house with children? I had a pretrial conference the next day and was sure I would be a hit with the judge.

Have you ever noticed that most little kids are cute? Like puppies and kitties, God made them that way as a means of survival. Otherwise, how can you accept waking up in the middle of the night to the sound of aboriginal screams coming from the nursery, changing dirty diapers, forgetting how to talk like an adult, and reading nighttime stories like *Goodnight Moon* to a child who has little desire to go to sleep and give you a couple hours of rest so you can do the dishes, wipe up the dinner that's splattered all over the floor, pick up the cars and trucks and My Little Pony pieces scattered all over the house, and color the premature gray roots in your part since you no longer have time to go to the hairdresser?

Anyway, back to *Goodnight Moon*. I had never heard of the book. Newly maternal Sherry claims this is a classic. I did verify that it was first published in 1947, so it has been around for a while. What normal mother lies in bed with her child and says goodnight to bears and chairs, kittens and mittens, clocks and socks, combs and brushes, and little houses and mouses? Good night, Miss Alice. Where was Ms. Brown born? It's almost impossible to believe that she's an American. I mean what American child is calmed by "goodnight mush"? Okay, maybe my son would have been more stable if I did the *Goodnight Moon* mush thing, but I wouldn't bet on it.

While I understand that Ms. Brown was not a Brit, she must have had some influences from across the pond. Not that Europeans are bad. My current husband is a Brit, and I love him dearly, but those that hale from across the pond are a little different from us normal folk here in the U.S. of A.

First, they say stupid things. What would you do if your thirteen-year-old daughter came home from school with that sick-ass puppy love look on her face and after a few prompts and prods gushes out,

"I shared a rubber with the new boy at school!"? Would your initial reaction be, at least she used protection and there are no questions about her sexuality? Not so much. You'd be on the phone to the principal in less than ten seconds demanding that the punk be expelled, and not until over forty minutes of nonstop ranting and raving do you take a breath long enough for the principal to say that the "new punk" hails from England and that Brits call erasers "rubbers." Now that sounds great and allows the blood pressure to drop to 180/100, but in the back of your mind, you still wonder whether it really was an eraser.

When I was in junior high and high school, I had little code words in my diary that I wrote faithfully every night to "Dear Jeannette." I had the code word ESW that really meant heavy fondling of my breasts. Extra ESW was moving further down below my navel, and the ultimate ESW was the real thing. How much did my mother really figure out when she would sneak a peek?

What if I was a grandmother and suddenly something dreadful happened to Alex, and his wife ran off with another man and left me with the children? What if I had to deal with a teenage daughter? You hear stories about couples in their sixties and seventies raising their grandchildren because their offspring went off the deep end due to the financial pressures in life and marriage or from smoking too much marijuana when teenagers.

Dealing with Sally CJ and Frances when they're in a dry spell is way easier than the thought of having to change diapers every day or deal with the trauma of a hormonal teenage daughter.

Never mind the Granny Laurie passing thought. Sherry's children refer to me as "Crazy Aunt Laurie," and that's sufficient. Graham and the sharks provide more than adequate fulfillment in life.

Women may be able to fake orgasms, but men can fake
whole relationships.

—*Sharon Stone*

Demons, Devils, and Other D Things

One of the hardest days in my life was when my dad died. We knew it was coming for years, but it was still very painful. My dad in a very quiet way was the cement that held a very fractured family together. With very little effort, my dad could make all other problems seem to be the size of a flea.

Dad called on Palm Sunday during the period when my son was the most obnoxious, therefore enabling Graham and me to be on a first-name basis with all the local police as well as the judges in the juvenile court system, and told me that God had spoken to him. Lovely. "Any what did God have to say?" I asked as the second unknown teenager dressed in all black skulked down the steps and out the front door at one thirty in the afternoon.

"God told me that I should no longer drive my car," Dad replied. In my heart of hearts, I knew that God was right. Even my teenage son would no longer ride in a car with his grandfather, not to baseball practice or to meet a friend to smoke weed at what was called band practice. But forget what was right; that was going to create one major problem if he was going to give up his only mode of transportation. How was he going to get to his weekly (gotta love Medicare) doctor appointments that were sixty miles away? Already the teenagers looming around the house and the acrid smell of cigarettes seemed to be a minor flash in the past.

"And, Samantha Laraine," he continued, "he told me to sell the house."

Oh, I knew that God was evil. "So," I stammered as a third punk came down the steps and had the audacity to ask if we had any Captain Crunch cereal, "where did God tell you to live?" I deferred the long-haired punk to the pantry.

"With you," my father announced.

Somehow I got off the phone and called my sister-in-law. "Help, God is talking to Pop."

"Please don't tell me he's having hallucinations," Marie moaned.

"I don't think so, but God told him to sell the house."

"Good, where did God tell him to live?" asked Marie.

"With us," I replied.

"Lovely," was her response.

And for the next four years, we shared my father. Or should I say, my sister-in-law and my husband shared my father, and Jonathan and I lived on airplanes in denial as we built up massive frequent flyer miles. Every time the plane pulled away from the gate, the sending party would sigh in exhaustion. Dad was a social butterfly without wings, which meant transporting him to bridge games, the library, and casinos for weekly challenges with the nickel video poker machines. He also sat at the head of the table for our monthly group dinner parties and loved every minute of it. Everyone loved my dad.

The end was as good as it gets. I flew to Nebraska to chill with Marie because even I felt that she was getting the bad end of the bargain. He had been living at an assisted living residence for about a year and was thriving, but the facility was less than a mile from her house, which meant daily visits to do laundry or sort pills or pay bills or just catch up on the gossip. At one point, Marie thought Marcia could pick up a sugar daddy there, but that concept vanished fast since few of the residents had a full set of permanent choppers.

The place definitely was not a pick-up joint, but it was a perfect venue for an aging parent who loved to tell the same stories about World War II over and over and over again. When the retired soldiers got together for dinner at the assisted living resort, they would tell their favorite war stories and then repeat the stories again the next night since they would be long forgotten, and the men would laugh with new zeal at the much told story the next day. The best part was that my dad could tell the best war stories, yet he spent most of the war at the University of West Virginia and never got further away than Fort Rucker. He had everyone convinced he participated in the Battle at Normandy. Guess bullshitting runs in the family.

This is advice for all of you who are struggling with aging parents who don't want to live at an assisted living residence. Pack their bags like you would send your reticent child to summer camp. All will be well. Do you remember the old Allan Sherman song, "Hello, Mother. Hello, Father. Here I am at Camp Grenada"? Find it and play it over and over and over again. It hits the nail on the head. Camp is good. Assisted living is like camp. Assisted living is good.

Everyone there loved my father, and during the last few days, they recalled delightful stories of the man we almost tried to forget. The last few days were peaceful and still typical of our noncommunicative family. Dad was in the process of dying, and we were gathered in Nebraska, hovering, waiting for the call, and reminiscing about our youth.

Marie had the best memory. It was a cold, rainy night in mid-April when she and Jonathan were first dating. They went back to the warm house for some heavy petting. Dad was half asleep and slumped down in his well-worn La-Z-Boy recliner with his favorite radio against his ear, listening to a late West Coast Oriole game. They were involved and unaware of his presence. A surprise grand slam homerun by Frank Robinson jarred Dad awake, and he was vaguely aware that his son was sitting on the couch. Being a little groggy, he didn't notice where Jonathan's hand was, so they were able to recover in time. By then, Dad, the consummate gentleman, realized Jonathan had a date, so he jumped up and extended his right hand to greet Marie. And there he was, standing in his white boxer shorts, welcoming the horrified twenty-year-old to his house. Over the years, we all got used to Dad tramping around the house in his white Jockeys.

We advised the hospice nurse not to call with "the news" from 10:00 p.m. to 8:00 a.m. since there were children to get to bed at night and off to school in the morning, and there was the adult late-evening wine tasting to help us get to the next day that did not need to be interrupted. After the kids were on the bus at 7:45 in the morning, we would stare at each other until 8:10 and then call in to see how Dad was. "Still hanging in there." No change on Wednesday. "Still hanging in there."

No change on Thursday. No change on Friday. He was just resting peacefully. Marie and I called the hospice nurse to get a better understanding of what was to come. It wasn't that we were eager for him to pass on, but we all needed guidance and some form of timeline.

The nurse was as surprised by his stamina as we were. "Is there anyone he hasn't spoken to?" she asked. We pondered, "No. He spoke to my husband and my son, and all the other family members have been by to see him." We were in a quandary. Dad seemed peaceful but clutched the bed rails in a death grip that signified incredible determination to stay in this world.

"What's keeping him here?" we kept asking ourselves.

"Fear of being with Mom?" I asked.

"Potentially," responded my brother.

"Fear of meeting up with Rags?" my sister-in-law offered. Rags was my mother's little rat dog who used to take flesh out of everyone within twenty yards, especially my father.

"That's another potential," I commented.

Friends would call and give us their family death and dying stories. Marie and I were hanging out at one of the Omaha hot spots, Blizzards. This is an ice cream parlor where the main fare is called a "concrete," meaning they cram as much ice cream and "goodies" in a container, thaw it, compact it, freeze it even more, and then hand you a Pepcid AC with the receipt.

One of Marie's friends, Charlotte, popped in after a hard workout session and after listening to our status report, sighed and in the longest southern drawl that obviously didn't come from a Midwest nasal tone upbringing said, "Oh, suggah, that's nothing. Let me tell y'all about the Summerville family tradition, which mind you, I plan on ending as soon as possible."

Oh, I bet this is a good one, I thought and buried my face in the important project at hand, shoveling vanilla ice cream with Heath Bar nuggets and sprinkles down my throat. What more could anyone tell us about the wishes of a dying family member?

"My Great-Aunt Clothilde always had a phobia about bugs," Charlotte began.

"Oh, this is really just what I wanted to hear as I looked at the tiny brown chunks in my ice cream."

"So," you couldn't help but wonder how she managed to make such a short word drag into three syllables, "she decided that she would be cremated to avoid the nasty potential of sharing her final resting place with bugs."

"Yeah, Graham and I are talking about the dust to dust approach also," I muttered as the ice cream delivered raging pain to my inner ear since it was too cold and I was inhaling it way too fast while trying to ignore the discussion.

"Well, honey, Great-Aunt C. was not just thinking of herself, she was setting in motion a family tradition. Her ashes were tinted purple during the cremation and placed in a large glass vase."

"Yuck!" She now had our attention.

"And Uncle John's ashes are on top of her ashes. They're deep red. Her sister, Minna, is now a lovely green, and her daughter, my Aunt Sue Ellen, is pink. Actually the pink is not much different from the deep red, but there's a timeline with color-coding taped to the vase to assist in making identification of family members when viewing the rainbow of dust."

"Wow, that's a real family tradition," said Marie as we stared at Charlotte, who was trying to file her thumb while clutching the concrete in her bulging bicep. She could never have been a real southern belle with arms like that.

"You win," I nodded. "You have the most dysfunctional family of all."

"Well, mah Ray, that's mah husband," she added for my benefit, "vowed as soon as he can get his hands on the vase, the tradition is over."

I wanted to ask whose fireplace mantle the vase was adorning, but Marie gave me one of those "shut your mouth" looks, and although I knew she was right, I couldn't control myself and blurted out, "I hope you're supporting him on this one." I remembered that Marie had described Charlotte's marriage to a Boston investment banker as a continuation of the Civil War.

"You bet your sweet lily white you know what, I am. I will take the maggots. No one is going to look at me in a jar. Besides, I wanted to be purple." Charlotte put away the nail file and began licking the concrete and sashayed out the door.

"Wow. Tell me that was a dream. She makes Sally CJ's screwed up family seem close to normal."

"Oh yeah. You never know what's going to come out of her mouth. I plan my workouts when I know she can't come to the gym. Try to picture her with our trainer now that he decided to be a she. Paul, oops Paula, is the old Paul and Paula song all in one. "

I had been there for nearly ten days, and it was time to get back to Graham and sex and work. We stopped by Dad's room, and I whispered that I was heading to the airport. Before I landed in Las Vegas, Marie called Graham to say that Dad was only waiting for me to get on a plane to go home, so he could do the same. Even in death, he was trying to hold the family together and avoid a family argument over the funeral and viewing arrangements.

The funeral. That was the next problem. The few people that were alive and had not lost their cognitive powers to Alzheimer's and still remembered my dad were on the East Coast. I was on the West Coast, and Marie and Jonathan were right smack in the middle. We finally decided to have a small service at Dad's assisted living home and ultimately have a service for neighbors and friends at the church where we grew up.

After spending two months comparing travel, vacation, and children's athletic activities, there were two weekends open, my birthday and my brother's birthday. This was the first coin toss I ever won, and so it was Jonathan who got to celebrate turning fifty at my dad's memorial service.

The day of the memorial service was the fifth day of solid rain. Living in the desert, I had nearly forgotten the phenomena and what it does to my hair. I spent two hours putting on makeup and teasing and spraying hair at the BWI Marriott, and I would have spent another two if I thought it would have helped. I knew we should have had the service in Las Vegas. Then I could have gone to Neiman's and had my makeup done right. This was a big event. Kind of like a high school reunion where I had to look good in case I ran into J. T. Harris, my seat mate in English who I always had a secret crush on. If only I had known the next sequence of events, I may not have opted for the age- and occasion-appropriate black suit with a high lacy collared blouse, no visible cleavage, i.e., an East Coast outfit.

By the time we ran from the car to the church, my hair looked like a mop. In fact, it looked just like it looked every Sunday when I was in high school trolling the church halls for a date. I stood in the bathroom, and the memories flooded through my mind. Sunday school with Fred Franklin, captain of the cross-country team; Friday night dances chasing one of the two-first-name wonders, James Allen, Steven George, Ronnie Andrew; sneaking a beer in the church balcony with the preacher's son; youth group retreats where even the counselors were in the sack with someone. Oh yes, the memories.

The minister of the church, who was well briefed on my dad's CV and former activities at the church, gave a very knowledgeable eulogy and then turned the service over to family and friends to share memories of my dad. There was a table at the front of the church where Marie placed Dad's picture and several other mementos—his dog's leash, family photos, a worn deck of playing cards, a hat from his favorite Las Vegas breakfast restaurant, and the program from the Colts-Giants NFL Championship Game on December 28, 1958, otherwise known as the Greatest Football Game Ever Played. Jonathan went up to the pulpit and began to share his memories with the forty family friends who came to pay respects. I had made it very clear that I was not going to speak. Speaking at memorial services is not my thing. In fact, public speaking when I haven't had several drinks and a glass of wine in my hand is not done outside the work environment. It just breeds trouble.

After I stopped daydreaming, I began to listen to what my brother was saying, and I began to squirm. Had we really lived in the same house? Did we both share the same parents? Wow. I just sat there convinced that I was at the wrong church. The difference in our ages and the world during which we grew up was staggering. I used to think I didn't like him. That's not the case because I had no idea who he was.

Several other family friends spoke for the next half hour. I looked at my watch several times because Marie had planned lunch for everyone at the local pub, and my salivary glands were starting to activate, and my stomach reminded me that I had not eaten anything due to the marathon makeup and hair session. The minister was starting to announce the final hymn when the devil took over, and I jumped up, grabbed the microphone, and said, "Not so fast." After all, a lawyer can never let an accountant type have the final word on anything. I then found myself staring at my past.

My dad's photograph from the 1969 church directory was focused in my direction, and when looking at my childhood friends as I started to correct Jonathan's childhood memories, all I could see were their parents. Sharon Jones, one of my cohorts in church misbehavior, looked just like her father; Carol Phelps, my old babysitter, looked just like her mother. It was like a time warp from the *Twilight Zone*. It was a challenge as I tried to speak coherently while stepping back in time more than forty years. Then my eyes scanned the back row. I tried not to squint. There were Hank and Sue Johnson, who looked exactly like their parents and now lived in Sue's parents' house two doors down from my old house. It was the recognition of the person sitting beside them, however, that caused the hair on my arms to rise to attention. I blubbered a few nonsensical words that my son said made perfect sense and sat down and stared off into space while everyone sang the closing hymn.

I was afraid to turn around. Alex said I looked green. Graham asked if I was okay. I nodded and walked to the back of the church toward Hank and Sue. Oh, my God, it was Fred Franklin, and he was smiling at me. The last time we spoke was when he told me that he was boycotting the senior prom as a protest to the Kent State police brutality. What did a senior prom have to do with the Vietnam War? As I now remember it, several graduates were recently killed in action, and the former captain of the football team was listed as MIA, and the senior class officers wanted to protest the war. Protests were one thing, but the senior prom was something else. I still get pissed just thinking of it. I devoted six months of my senior year in high school freezing my ass off at cross-country meets cheering him on. All for what? No date to the senior prom. And there he was smiling at me. He had aged well, very well.

I just stood there, mouth open, no words forthcoming. It was just like the day I finally met my idol, Jim Palmer, number 22 of the Baltimore Orioles. My beloved Jim pitched for the Orioles from 1965 to 1984, and I lusted after him long after that. Every time I got in an airplane, I would pray that my seatmate would be Jim Palmer, not the greasy, three-hundred-pound Italian dockworker I usually ended up sitting beside. When I married Graham, I told him that I would be faithful to him unless Jim Palmer or Kevin Costner wanted to replicate the famous love scene in *An Officer and a Gentleman*. Graham sensed that there was little risk of that happening and bought in.

Many years ago, we went to an Oriole game in Cleveland, and Brooks Robinson, third base, number 5, and Jim Palmer were doing the television commentary. We went to the stairs by the TV booth and waited. Brooks came first, and I chatted with him for a while. Old ball players are easy to talk to and enjoy chatting it up with former fans. Then I caught Jim Palmer coming down the stairs; he came closer, and there he was. He sat his briefcase down and came over to chat with the several fans standing around. He walked straight up to me and said, "Hello." I opened my mouth—and nothing. That's right, nothing came out. He gave me a strange look, and before he could turn toward Graham, I blurted out, "I like your tie, Mr. Palmer."

Can you believe it? For over forty years, I have been fantasizing over this guy who's only a couple years older than I am, certainly younger than many of my conquests, and all I can say is, "I like your tie, Mr. Palmer. " Not even, "Do you want to fuck?" which believe you me I have thought about many times. Not even, "Do you still wear jockey underwear? I loved you in those canary yellows." No, all I can say is, "I like your tie, Mr. Palmer."

Well, there I am in front of Fred Franklin, and I start to speak, and he says, "Do you remember me?"

I began to respond when Carole Carlton walks up and says, "Fred, what are you doing here? I didn't know you knew Mr. Anderson." The sight of Carole Carlton almost made me puke. There's one in every class, the girl who started wearing a bra in the fifth grade and by the seventh grade could have had a role in a B movie. From what I understand, it would have been *Deep Throat* by the way. The long, blonde hair was now red, and her 34C was at least a double D, and there was not an ounce of fat on her body. We used to call her the "terminator" since she was responsible for the breakup of couples throughout history, including my short-lived romance with Dick Hall. Oh, Carole Carlton, a sight for sore eyes.

Fred slid closer, put his arm on my shoulder, and said, "Carole, Laurie was my first girlfriend." He then turned to me and said, "Carole is my wife's sister." I guess "the terminator" left family member's spouses alone.

My heart was thumping, and I could only pray that it wasn't audible. "So you were waiting for me all those years?" I cooed, blatantly ignoring Carole. Fred responded, "Something like that," and dropped his arm around my waist.

He introduced himself to Graham and asked Graham if he minded if he gave me a tour of changes in the church. Graham nodded sure, and I began to sweat. Graham didn't have a clue what that meant and smiled as we strolled off together.

Fred was describing the new stained-glass window when I glanced over my shoulder and saw Carole hanging on Graham. I saw his eyes lock on to her cleavage and turned my attention back to Fred. I knew where the church tour was heading, to the church bowling alley. That's right; our church has a bowling alley that was often referred to as Make-Out Alley or Lovers' Lane. Oh boy. One more glance at Graham, and he was definitely taking all of Carole in. You go, girl. Graham was occupied.

There we were. The lane had not seen action for years, and the pins were toppled over, but the cove around the corner was still there, just like

I remembered it. "I still think of you, and when I saw the notice in the church bulletin that your Dad passed away, I felt a need to see you again."

Another happy marriage. Was my former area of expertise being rekindled at church? Was this God's wish or was it the devil? "What's Carole doing here?" My breathing wasn't steady.

"She's been after me for years, and Sue didn't want to come to the service, so I guess Carole just stopped by to keep me company. I forgot you knew her."

Yeah right, I thought.

"So," he said as I was pinned against the wall between still firm arms. "We sure had a great time here during our senior year, didn't we?" With that, he leaned in for a kiss, and I was going to have to make a quick decision. This was not going to end in just a kiss. My body was telling me that, and Fred was not on the allowable fuck list. I didn't have an allowable make-out list so I was in a gray area.

Voices. It was Alex and his cousin. "Wow. A bowling alley at church. That's cool."

"Hi, guys. I want you to meet an old friend. Fred, my son and nephew." In my frustration, I gave no names and fled back to the sanctuary.

Fred came to the luncheon, and when everyone was saying their good-byes, he came up and kissed me firmly on the lips and brushed his hand against my breast. I melted. "Call me if you get back in town. I'm in the book," he said as he waved from the door. I don't remember if I ever got that far in high school with him. I think he was saving it for the prom that never happened.

I guess the devil lives somewhere deep down inside all of us, and old demons and desires from our youth never quite go away.

If only one could tell true love from false love as one
can tell mushrooms from toadstools.

—Katherine Mansfield

Is it a Dream Date or a Backdoor Exit?

"So I still think it's hypocritical," Sue said as she rolled her eyes. I met Sue at the gym, and she's a hoot. She used to be a dancer in one of the shows on the strip. She maintains that she lost her job because she was the only one in the chorus line with real boobs. Her husband of twenty years just left her to fondle a silicone-injected teenager on a nightly basis, and she's less than pleased with her new lifestyle.

"Nothing is as it seems. What difference does it make?" Frances slurred as she put her glass down, and the golden colored liquid sloshed over the side onto the checkered tablecloth. Frances was in town visiting me after another fiasco on match.com.

"Yeah, but a Cosmo is red, not yellow," Sue argued as she slugged down her second Guinness.

"We all can agree that men are liars and cheats, and my favorite drink now looks like pee. How rude," Frances moaned.

"What's up, bitch?" my new neighbor Margo said as she slid in the booth next to me.

"Sue went on another date last night, and it didn't go too well. Then she ordered a Cosmo, and it was yellow. The bartender called it a Golden Cosmo. He said they ran out of cranberry juice last night, and he was being creative. I switched to Guinness when I saw it."

"That's pretty lame. So who was the guy," Margo asked. "Are you still using match.com after Phil?

"The concept of never having sex after fifty makes you do stupid things, Margo. You wouldn't know though. I saw the Boxter in front of your house last Saturday night when I was leaving Laurie's house."

"Yeah, but you didn't see the cane, did you? My boss set me up with his wife's brother, and now I'm totally fucked. When the Boxter man called to arrange the date, he warned me that he injured his ankle and was temporarily using a cane."

"Not a big deal. Graham ripped his hamstring playing tennis last summer, and it had minimal effect on his you know what," I chimed in.

"Well, this guy may not even have a you-know-what because we didn't get that far, and I don't care how he got home from the Sharkey's or how he got his car on Sunday or if he's even alive." Margo appeared to be bitter.

Sharkey's is a small restaurant about three miles from our house where the girls often go for drinks to check out blind-date candidates. Joe, the bartender, keeps an eye on us and lets us out the back door when we get stuck with a real loser. "Wait a minute. Slow down. How did you get to Sharkey's if Mr. Porsche didn't drive?"

"I'm such an ass. Everyone's been taking pity on me since Joe left, and since my boss vetted him, I thought he could just come over, and we could sit on the patio and have a drink and appetizers. I felt bad he was injured and didn't want him hobbling around on the strip on a Saturday night." Margo is another single divorcee in Las Vegas.

"So." Frances is always interested in a Porsche man but personally prefers the 911 type of guy. "What went wrong?"

"Well, unless you go on Medicare at the age of fifty-four in Boston, the guy is more of a fraud than the Golden Cosmo you're drinking."

"A little age misrepresentation, eh?" I asked.

"He had to have been seventy, if not closer to eighty. It's one thing to take a couple years off, but a generation is going a little too far. This guy had to have been my boss's wife's father."

Frances shook her head. "We need more respect. Do we appear to be so desperate for a guy that a friend would to try to dump his wife's dad on us? Maybe your boss doesn't like you."

"And the battery died on his hearing aid, so he had to just about sit on my lap to carry on a discussion. That way I could get a real good look at the brown age spots on his hands. Worse yet, I think the Boxter was a rental because I don't think he's a local."

"Loser," chimed in Sue.

"So how did the car wind up in front of your house the next day? Do penises get age spots?"

"Go to hell. I told him I ran out of tonic, and I drove us to Sharkey's for a drink. Then after hearing about the pitfalls of Medicare and the lack of insurance for senior citizens, I had to visit the ladies' room, and Joe let me out the backdoor escape hatch. I have no idea when he came by for the car, but I assume I'm out of a job tomorrow."

"Good riddance," chimed in Sue. "By the way, Frances, I'm looking for someone to go to Australia with me next month. I have tons of miles on United and will treat you."

"Don't do it," I moaned. "Did you hear what happened when Frances went to Sydney with Graham and me last year?"

"Frances went to Sydney with you and Graham?" Margo asked.

"Yeah, we were visiting friends we met at the Olympics in 2000, and the next thing we knew, she was nearly in the sack with our host's daughter's boyfriend."

"That's an exaggeration," Frances said, not making eye contact. "He was cute and was a chef and was teaching me how to make pizza."

"You were getting too close to the pepperoni and almost caused an international incident."

"Yeah, I did make a mistake. I thought what goes on in Sydney stays in Sydney."

"Maybe, but not with our hosts' future son-in-law."

"Well, nothing happened."

"Yeah, but only because of the eight-inch spider," I replied.

"Is that what they call them Down Under? How clever." Margo was hooked.

"No, asshole. Not dicks. There was a real spider on the bathroom wall when Frances was touching up her makeup before the seduction. This hairy creature was hanging on the bathroom mirror, and Frances starting screaming so loud everyone in the house came running. Fortunately, if her dress was off as Graham and I suspect, she managed to get it back on before the crowd arrived, and she miraculously explained away why she was in Evan's bathroom."

"Wow. Never slept with an Aussie before," sighed Sue.

"I heard everything is bigger is Australia," chirped Frances, "but I can only vouch for spiders."

"Sue. Don't listen to Frances. The guy was from Spain, not Australia, so she wouldn't know anything about the private parts of an Aussie," I said.

"Boring," sighed Sue. "Maybe we can find out about native Aussies next month. Think about it."

"Doesn't anyone care about my disastrous date?" whined Frances.

"Sure, can't be worse than my last foray on the dating scene, which was also a blind date set up by a so-called friend," Margo said, shaking her head. "The guy was a sports agent for some baseball farm team on the East Coast and claimed he knew Jim Palmer."

My ears perked up. "Jim Palmer. I love Jim Palmer. Graham said I can sleep with Jim Palmer. I'm sure that's because he must be approaching sixty-five, but Cakes is still Cakes. I may be happily married but can feel that warm sensation down under when I hear his name and ponder the old Jockey underwear ads. God, it ages me."

"Well, did you know that Jim Palmer and all the Orioles used to call Earl Weaver 'Rooney,' like in Mickey Rooney?" Margo continued in a nonchalant tone.

God, Margo had the next best thing to the dream date and was bitching.

"And did you know that when it appeared that Jim Palmer was getting lax and letting runners get on base so Weaver would have pitchers start warming up in the bull pen, it was really just to piss him off?"

I can no longer stand it. "What the fuck is wrong with you?" I screamed.

It was like saying "E. F. Hutton" in the commercials. There was complete silence in the restaurant. "You need to marry the guy."

"Your dream date clipped his fingernails after his appetizer."

My blood is still rushing. "So what's a minor fetish? He didn't eat them, did he?" Imagine, Margo and Mr. Sports Agent can have Cakes over for an outdoor BBQ, and I can hop over the ten-foot wall separating our houses and fulfill my fantasy.

"Well, as a matter of fact, he did, and I was out of there. Besides, Jim Palmer is married, and so are you."

Obviously we cannot rely on blind dates set up by friends, and the results from Frances's Internet cross-examination techniques leave much to be desired. How do we screen out the old fossils, the nail clippers, and the deaf and blind?

We need a new list. Margo pulled out a napkin and wrote down the following New Rules:

Always obtain a photo before a visual encounter.

After Sally CJ had the run-in with the guy with the bad teeth, we learned to require a photo with a smile.

In fact, don't stop with a headshot. Go for a full frontal view. There are a lot of nasty things that can be hidden between the chin and the navel.

Beware; it is easy to post a photo that's a decade old. Frances used that trick often.

To eliminate a midget you will tower over in your stilettos, make sure he stands in front of a railing or other fixture you can use as a benchmark to judge height.

Easiest solution is to require a photo taken on the beach beside the life guard stand with the dude wearing a Speedo and holding a copy of the Sunday paper showing the date to his side.

But the best no-fail solution is to meet the new candidate at a restaurant where you know there's a backdoor escape hatch.

A man in the house is worth two in the street.

—Mae West

Do Thrusters or Tuckers Make Better Lovers?

The other day, I was joking at my health club with my favorite boys, my trainer, my boxing coach, and my masseur, all under the age of twenty-seven and in perfect physical condition.

This is good. Several years ago, I got frustrated that movie stars and other very famous people around my age were still in fantastic shape, and my husband commented that it was part of their job to be in shape and they worked very hard at maintaining less than 20 percent body fat. Well, I considered myself to be a princess, so why should I be packing an extra 15–20 percent of fat that wasn't located on my bust line? If princesses were expected to work out in a gym with a trainer, why shouldn't I do the same?

We've been brainwashed that thin is good. I was born a size eight, so you can say I was fucked at birth because that didn't leave much room to grow. I obviously didn't take after my mother who never wore maternity clothes and was on a forced milkshake diet during pregnancy with me. Even when I was my leanest in high school, weighing 115 pounds, Mom chided me about my thunder thighs. I think I was programmed to be bulimic, which I was throughout college and into my early thirties.

Girls today complain about the waifs and Kate Moss; well, we had Twiggy, all bones and fake eyelashes. My dream is that Queen Latifah and James Earl Jones will replace Ken and Barbie as the true American Idols. Can you imagine what their offspring would look like! Good-bye form-fitting clothes. Think about the Queen as a role model and the new size standard. Good-bye, Weight Watchers, hello, Baskin Robbins. Just thinking about it makes me want to break into the Haagen Dazs.

It all started on Groundhog Day. All eyes were on Tony Perkins, the weatherman on *Good Morning America*, as he stood in the freezing cold beside a fake burrow in Punxsutawney, Pennsylvania, waiting patiently for the rodent to emerge from his cozy little home. I was getting dressed and looked in the bathroom mirror and realized that my physique bore a real resemblance to a groundhog and decided that I needed to take aggressive action. Tony Perkins announced that the little bastard didn't see his shadow, and that meant summer was six weeks closer and getting into size ten bathing suit was not going to be an easy proposition. I wasn't even certain that a size twelve wasn't going to rip at the seams if I tried to swim a lap in the pool.

I've always been honest in admitting what size bathing suit I wear. In general, it's a size twelve unless I opt for a Gottex, and then I can cram my butt into a ten. Obviously, that means I'm willing to shell out $150 for a Gottex rather than $60 for other brands. A girl has to have some pride.

I have a girl friend who I know is larger than I am, and she maintains that she's a size eight, a Gottex size eight, but no matter how you cut it, eight, a single digit. I know bathing suits stretch a lot, but when I put on an eight, it gives a new meaning to the terms "girdle" and "flabby overhang." No way. I cannot breathe. Maybe she views it as an alternative to a diet. If you wedge your body into an eight and wear it from when you get up in the morning until dinnertime, there's no way you can overeat. No thank you.

Anyway, it was the bathroom scene that drove me to the health club. "I need the best trainer on the staff," I stated emphatically.

"We have a staff of twelve trainers, and they're all excellent."

"Okay, then give me the cutest trainer on your staff."

"That's not exactly how it works. We need to perform an assessment of your physical condition and health goals, and then we decide which trainer can best assist you in achieving those objectives."

Wait a minute. I'm going to pay fifty-five dollars an hour, and I'm going to have some chick working in a sales office determine who's going to train me?

"What do you think this is—a trainer matchmaker service?"

"We need to establish your profile."

"My profile is that I'm fat and I need to lose some pounds and reduce my body fat quickly, and I want to enjoy looking at the person who's going to put me through the painful process."

After an hour of arguing, I was assigned to Marcus. I knew that bitch hated me because Marcus was not in the top ten. I work out in a gym where the average age is less than twenty-five, and the typical employment for women is showgirl or stripper. I can tell because when they lay down on the floor to do crunches, their boobs point up like lampposts. I also observed that the good-looking trainers were training the showgirls, and the female trainers and the older male trainers with a paunch had the senior citizens and the walruses that were not going to last long. That's age and weight discrimination for sure.

I was committed to improving my body, so I wanted one of the hunks.

Marcus and I lasted two sessions. I knew it was over day one, but he felt we could work it out. I'm strong and wasn't going to tolerate doing bicep curls using three-pound weights. Session two, we focused on legs, and he had me doing leg extensions with ten pounds. I flipped the weight up to thirty, and he walked off, yelling, "Who's training who?" over his shoulder.

"That's whom!" I yelled back. Asshole cannot even speak good English.

I went over to the sales staff and demanded a new trainer. I had prepaid for sixty sessions, and I knew they didn't want to give me a refund. This time I got Jeanine.

Jeanine was a nice girl and really wanted to work with me. We worked together for three days, but she admitted that we weren't a match made in heaven.

John was the next trainer.

"No one else has this much trouble finding a trainer," exclaimed the Fitness Manager (otherwise known around the gym as the FM).

By this point, I had checked out all of the bodies on the staff and knew who it would be. "I want him," I said, pointing across the gym.

"That's Parker. He is our elite trainer."

Parker. The name sounded right out of Beverly Hills. "Yeah, well I'm an elite kinda girl."

"No," explained the FM. "He works with clients who are professionals and need to keep in shape for their job."

"Yeah, the lap dancers. Well, tell him he has to do his time with the old lady."

We hit it off immediately. I told him my goals and said I would work as hard as he pushed me. I told him that I didn't want to be treated like an old lady.

I did an hour of cardio, and then we headed over to the weights. I'm sure he was primed by Marcus because he started off with bicep curls using fifteen-pound weights. The guy was not going to make me wimp out. I matched him set for set the first thirty minutes. Finally, I was exhausted. He added another ten pounds to the lat pull down machine, and I broke. "Fuck you. You win." As the final "ou" was coming out of my mouth, there wasn't a sound to be heard in the gym, and all those nineteen-inch waists were giving me that "Give it up, you fat old cow" look.

Now I was fucked.

"I will be delighted to train you." Wow. "But only on one condition. We back off a little bit on the weights, but I promise that you'll leave the gym exhausted every time we train."

This began my relationship with Parker. For the past two years, he has been busting my chops three to four times a week with weights and demanding that I do cardio on the weekend when we don't train. And cardio did not mean using the Precor Elliptical machine; it meant fighting off all the dancers for the Stair Master, a guaranteed heart attack. I know if I didn't consume so much Guinness and Bordeaux, I would be as svelte as Goldie Hawn. However, a senior princess does have priorities.

Parker has decided that this is the year of the "glutes," as in ass, and we have devoted at least ten minutes four days a week to firming it up. This is not easy work. The concept is not much different from trying to get Jell-O to be as hard as concrete. I think the likelihood of Parker creating buns of steel on this body is as probable as me getting a date with Kevin Costner.

"Do you know what your problem is?" Parker asked one day as I was moaning extra loudly while doing squats.

"Yeah. My problem is that I need a new trainer who's not obsessed with pain. That's my problem at this moment."

"No, I've been watching you, and your problem is that you're a tucker."

"A what?"

"You're a tucker, and most women are thrusters."

"Come again?"

"Most women are butt thrusters, and you're a butt tucker," and he began to demonstrate the differences in butt techniques.

"Well, you're a penis pointer," I retaliated. I was not going to be called a tucker.

I thought he was going to pee in his pants. Not everyone has a relationship with his or her trainer like I do with Parker. Even though I'm old enough to be his mother, he treats me like one of his peers. I know it's because I work my ass off in the gym five days a week, but it's one of the few times that I forget about my age.

I was sharing the thrusting, tucking, pointing session with Sally CJ, and she clearly agreed that most men are penis pointers, because they lead with their number-one brain, but she wondered whether tuckers or thrusters made better fuckers. I think she's going to take a poll at her office since most of the instructors at the junior college where she's a dean are men under the age of thirty.

Then she said she wants to meet Parker the next time she comes to town. I don't think so. I've told Parker Sally CJ stories, and I cannot afford to add my trainer to the endangered species list.

A few months ago, Parker decided that I needed to insert some variety in my training program, and he introduced me to Henry the Boxer—no shit, a real, former professional boxer. I think it was an attempt to give me an outlet for my aggression so I'd drop the F word from my workouts.

Boxing is great! It's a great alternative to drinking if you're not getting enough sex. Since Frances's consumption level is on the rise, I need to get her into this sport.

Boxing is a lot harder than it appears. During my first session, Henry began giving me the basic guidelines. "Your left hand is one, and your right hand is two. When I say 'one,' hit my left glove with your left hand, and when I say 'two,' hit my right glove with your right hand. Got it?"

"Yo, I'm good to go."

"One." I hit his left glove.

"Two." I hit his right glove.

And so it went: one, punch; one, punch; two, punch; two, punch; one, two, punch, punch. This was cool. I started dancing from side to side. "Whoa, what's that?" he asked.

"Man, I'm the great Mohamed Ali, and I'm dancing like a butterfly and stinging like a bee!"

"Just plant your feet and hit my glove. One-two, one-two, one, one—"

Crack! I got carried away and forgot my numbers and landed a right fist right on his jaw instead of the left hand jab to his glove. Man, there was blood.

"Ahhhh. I'm so sorry. Really, I just lost count. It seemed like it was time for a two."

"I'm okay," Henry grimaced. "That was a good one, but try to pay attention."

I guess I shouldn't tell him that ADD runs in the family. I'm getting better and only hit him every other session, but now he's prepared and wears a mouth guard.

One day, I complained to Henry that I was sore, so he introduced me to Harris, the massage guy. Harris is another hard body who takes his job and profession very seriously. Deep tissue massages are not for the weak. They're painful. But how often can a woman my age have Adonis rub her back with only a sheet separating her naked body from him? So I did what any rational woman with an American Express card would do. I prepaid for twenty sessions and got four massages for free. That's nearly a year's worth of fondling according to my calculations.

Sally CJ dared me to kick off the sheet. I think Harris has a way to go before I take the challenge to find out. I'm afraid he'll refund my money if I dare to suggest that more than a massage would be a good thing. Sally CJ isn't taking "I can't do that" for an excuse. I'm afraid she's going to come to town and ruin my relationship with the boys.

God, my husband is a saint! I still don't know the answer to Sally CJ's question about tuckers and thrusters, but I do know my body fat is less than twenty-two and heading in the right direction.

> *God made man stronger but not necessarily more*
> *intelligent. He gave women intuition and femininity.*
> *And used properly, that combination easily jumbles the*
> *brain of any man I've ever met.*
>
> *—Farrah Fawcett*

The C Word

"High-grade epidermoid carcinoma" is what the preliminary biopsy read. What the fuck does that mean? I was sitting in the concierge lounge at the Ritz Carlton back East on one of my semiannual junkets trying to shake down my deep-pocket clients so I could pay off mounting credit card debt that I had been hiding from my husband when my cell phone blasted out the old Baltimore Colts marching song. I may be a Ravens fan, purple face, hard hat with purple feathers adorned with a massive Edgar Allan Poe raven (actually I think it's a crow), but some traditions will never die. Thank God the Ravens' organization finally adopted the old Colts' song with an update in words.

The Baltimore Colts, the good old days. I grew up suffering from my parents abandoning me on Sunday afternoons from September through December to cheer the likes of Johnny Unitas, Raymond Berry, Lenny Moore, Alan Ameche, Gino Marchetti, and of course, Big Daddy Lipscomb while they perched in section 5, row G, seats 1 and 2, just under cover may I add, at Memorial Stadium. In today's world, parents take their children to sporting events. I think this is what we now refer to as a family outing. Not in my family.

Share football tickets with the children? The idea was blasphemous. Did you ever see June and Ward Cleaver take the Beaver to an NFL football game? No way. Well, that was how it was. The only time in my entire youth that my parents were willing to share those blue and white tickets with the upside-down golden horseshoe was the day my mother had a 103 degree temperature, and the thermometer on the patio was hovering around five degrees, and the wind was so strong that the limbs on the forty-year-old oak trees in the front yard were parallel to the white fence rails.

After I got home from Sunday school, Dad asked the unthinkable, "Would you like to take a friend to the Colts game today?" Wow! Of course. No more cheering to the crackling radio. I called my best friend, Barb, and in less than two hours of prep time, we were ready. We had on our best Villager slacks, penny loafers (with stockings, of course), and our pea coats. "No, Mom, I'm not going to wear your stupid fur-lined stadium boots. Socks? No way. Gloves? How queer." Barb almost lost her big toe to frostbite. They didn't explain dressing for football games under arctic conditions in *Seventeen* magazine. Maybe there were grounds for some legal action, and we were too naive to know it.

Anyway, my first trade for sex as a maturing young woman was access to Colts season tickets in row 37 on the thirty-five-yard line. That's the row where men don't bother to trudge down the step to relieve themselves after the sixth beer. Au contraire, that was the row where they turned away from the field, whipped out the little wiener, and urinated for what seemed like half a quarter over the top of the stadium. Prime seats.

As the years progressed, I was able to legitimately trade down until I finally achieved the ultimate goal for any sports fan—lower upper-deck seats on the fifty-yard line. That was what life was all about. *Then* my entire levelheaded, antiviolence upbringing came to a halt. First I had to deal with the worst coach in the NFL, Mr. Run Up the Middle, Run Up the Middle, Run up the Middle, Punt, Ted Marchibroda. And if that wasn't the worst, I had "Why Won't Someone Shoot Him" Robert Irsay for an owner. The pair was a made-in-hell combination that resulted in an empty stadium by the fourth quarter of each home game and the infamous Mayflower moving van that raped the fine citizens of Baltimore in the early dawn on a snowy March 29, 1984.

True fans never forget, just like in the movie *Diner*. The Colts were all that was good in the sixties and seventies, and just like some of us still listen to the oldies station on the radio, some of us will never forget the Baltimore Colts and the day of reckoning.

I was just in the middle of a relatively nice cabernet when "Let's Go, You Baltimore Colts," oops, "Ravens" chimed on my cell phone. Very annoyed at the interruption—Survivor was just getting hot—I noted that it was my husband and knew he would only interrupt the squabbling of Gerry and Anita and the rest of the tribe if there was a reason. Well, he was going to have a small cyst removed from his neck the next day, and maybe he wanted a little comfort before undergoing the knife.

Everything was in place. The surgery was routine. He would stay overnight, and a girl friend (mine, not his) would take him home on Friday, and I would be home to play Nurse Nancy over the weekend. The health care directive was properly witnessed. All do-not-resuscitate orders were clear; if patient will drool, do not resuscitate. I'm sorry; I have this vision of my husband with a drool cup strapped around his neck to catch the uncontrollable slobber. I think the vision comes from an old *Saturday Night Live* show.

To me, that's adequate grounds to begin the search for husband number six. I don't consider it to be coldhearted, just realistic. I married a proper Brit, not a St. Bernard. In fact, just the thought gives new meaning to the phrase "uncontrollably running your mouth."

"My surgery is postponed," my husband blurted out. "I have cancer."

The C word.

Fuck me.

Fuck Robert Irsay.

Fuck the world.

The next weeks went by like a blur. Tests, tests, and more tests. Words like high-grade epidermoid carcinoma were rapidly added to our vocabulary. We learned what a PET scan was. No. It is not a new method for flea removal. It's a $3,000 test where you're injected with glucose and radionuclides to seek out cancer cells. Fleas, cancer, what's the difference? Both are hard to shake and need to be killed. Bob Irsay was a cancer to the City of Baltimore. Come to think of it, during those days, I was mesmerized by the book *Day of the Jackal* and could not understand why the Jackal was never recruited to remove the disastrous owner of the Colts.

Well, Dr. Doom is the Jackal of cancer. He was the medical oncologist assigned to eradicate the "monster bastard" growing on Graham's parotid gland and the "Taliban" hiding in his lower back. Those of you with any knowledge of anatomy must be thinking, *We're in trouble, girlfriend.*

Parotid is synonymous with drool. That's right, the parotid gland is the salivary gland, and we're now in butting up against the advanced health care medical directive regarding when to not resuscitate. Doctors have verified that the directive is valid. Yes, I love Graham dearly, but as Dr. Doom rapidly realized, caregiver is not listed in the description of personality traits of an attorney. We are trained to annihilate the weak, not change drool cups.

This causes great concern to Dr. Doom. His real name is Dr. Nick Dinacopoulous, but after our first meeting, we named him Dr. Doom because of his less than optimistic outlook on the potential of survival. I already knew that, but Graham the Brit was still living in the world of Harry Potter, so he had not focused on what the Google searches on the Internet were projecting for our future.

Graham was determined and upbeat—kinda like William the Conqueror, Mighty Mouse, Crusader Rabbit, and Super Chicken all rolled up in one. I was more like George of the Jungle, flying high for a few moments and then splatting into a tree for a touch of reality the next. We all have role models with whom we identified from childhood. Thank you, Mom and Dad.

Graham even sends out e-mails to his closest friends describing the "cancer process" and effects so that others can make a rational decision on whether or not he or she would rather blow off chemo and spend the rest of his or her life drinking and fucking on a beach.

Here's a typical e-mail:

To: Chosen Friends

Subject: The wonderful world of chemistry

I have now discovered that chemotherapy provides a classic example of chemical dependency that I previously thought was associated only with recreational drugs.

Knowing that assaulting your body with destructive drugs will produce any number of a long list of side effects, the medical profession stands ready with yet another pill to knock that one down. The weird thing is that the side effects seem to take their turn in manifesting themselves so you keep having to check back.

I have run through several of them already and will spare you the details. The doctors have done a good job of controlling the nausea etc. with preemptive doses, and I am grateful for that. I get antinausea medication in every infusion, and they have given me samples of a drug named Kytril that I take for the next three days that worked well in Round One anyway. Last Saturday was the day that the hair started to fall out in clumps, so today I went and had the whole head buzzed. I had my glasses off while it was done, and afterward when I looked in the mirror, I did not recognize the person looking back. Very weird! The next round will be the body hair—what a mess!

The overall effect of this therapy feels not unlike being given a case of the flu. Many of the same symptoms but overall a general loss of energy that takes awhile to get used to.

Round Two starts tomorrow, and I suspect that the cumulative effects will be a little rougher than the first time around. I hope to know whether the doctor is able to tell if the tumor has been reduced at all. It seems to have become a little smaller to my touch, but maybe it's just wishful thinking. If these drugs are beating the crap out of me this bad, they sure as hell better be beating it up too.

Everything is day-to-day, but today I feel pretty good overall. Fortunately, I am able to work okay and am able to do a fair amount via the use of e-mail etc. I am actually expecting that tomorrow I will be doing some billable work while receiving the chemotherapy. Let's hope I can keep it going.

Amazing.

Just reading the e-mail shows the difference between the determined and those that need an excuse to drink themselves to oblivion.

The minute I met Dr. Doom, I knew that the cancer was fate and that our paths were meant to cross. He was a Hunk, with a capital H! I would have preferred that we met at the gym rather than at the Cancer Institute, but that's life. *Ewewewewewe,* bad choice of words.

At the news of the cancer, Sally CJ was besieged with worry. Graham couldn't be sick; she was going to marry him. I told her not to fear, and I told her about the unmarried Dr. Doom. Sally CJ replied, "I can do Greeks." Now that causes me a slight problem. I'm already on a mission to find an eligible Greek for one of my clients, so I have a potential conflict. I called Frances for either advice or to add her to the bachelorette list since Dr. Doom has a full head of hair, a full set of bleached teeth, and runs in 10K races in between developing chemo cocktails for the unsuspecting.

Frances informed me that she already tried to do a Greek, and she wasn't interested and insisted that I should not worry because Sally CJ would not "do Greeks" either. I didn't believe it, but she told me to check my e-mail in an hour because she had firsthand knowledge of the complications associated with a non-Greek getting seriously involved with a true Greek.

An hour later, my computer choked out the following recipe:

Mageritsa (Easter Lamb Soup)

Ingredients:

Intestines, heart, lungs, and liver of 1 lamb

1	Lamb's feet and tripe
1	Lamb's head
	Salt
2	Lemons (juice only)
1	small bunch scallions, chopped
2/3 c	Chopped fresh parsley
1/2 c	Chopped fresh dill
1/4 c	Chopped celery leaves
6 T	raw long-grain white rice
1/2 t	Aniseed
	Freshly ground pepper
3	Whole eggs

Note: If using the lamb's head, wash it and then soak it in cold water for three hours. Drain. Cut the head in half, using a sharp knife, and tie with a clean string.

Prepare lamb's feet and tripe as follows: If tripe is not partially cooked, cut open with a sharp knife and clean the inside thoroughly under running water. Put in a pan with cold, salted water to cover and soak for thirty minutes. Then drain and wash with cold water. Cut into small pieces and put in a large soup pot with the lamb's feet. Cover with cold water and simmer until tender, adding salt to taste during the last minutes of cooking. Cube the tripe, remove the meat of the feet from the bones, and add to the mageritsa at the same time as the cut-up intestines, adjusting the liquid by adding more water.

Clean the intestines thoroughly by turning them inside out, using a long skewer or stick (this turning will be quicker if the intestines are first cut into two-foot lengths), and then wash under cold running water until clean. Rub the intestines with salt and the juice of half a lemon, rinse again in cold water, and drain. Braid the intestines. Put in a large soup pot with the lamb's head and cover with cold water. Bring to a boil, and then lower the heat, skim, and simmer for thirty minutes.

Remove the intestines, drain them, and cut into quarter-inch pieces with the scissors and set aside to add to the soup later. (Use the remaining portion of the head for another dish.) Bring the soup stock to a boil and add the scallions, parsley, dill, and celery leaves. Cut the heart, lungs, and liver into small bite-sized cubes and add them to the soup, and simmer for fifteen minutes. Add the rice, cut-up intestines, aniseed, salt and pepper to taste and continue simmering until the rice is tender, approximately fifteen minutes, adding more water as needed and the brains during the last few minutes of cooking.

Half an hour before serving, bring the soup to a boil. Then remove from the heat and prepare the avgolemono: Beat the eggs for two minutes. Continue to beat and gradually add the remaining lemon juice. Then one to two, cups of the hot soup by droplets, beating steadily, until all has been added. Add the avgolemono to the soup. Stir over minimum heat until thickened. Serve warm but avoid boiling the soup after adding the avgolemono.

And people call that appetizing?

Frances had been dating Alex the Greek for over a year when he asked her to meet the family for Easter dinner. She knew it was going to be the day he finally popped the Big Question and, wearing a new Chanel suit and matching pumps that cost her the next year's salary, eagerly anticipated becoming Mrs. Alex Milikinos. When they walked into the house, her gag reflex jumped into high gear. There had to be a dead body stuffed in the closet. Never had she smelled anything as foul as the odor coming from the kitchen.

"Dinner is about to be served. Please, my dear, come to the table and meet the family."

As she and Alex entered the dining room, thirty family members were already seated, and Mrs. Milikinos was serving soup. The nauseating smell was the soup. All eyes were on her. Everyone knew she was not Greek, but she was not going to succumb to the pressure. She accepted her serving, closed her eyes, and joined the family slurping.

As the liquid would go down and then bubble back up her esophagus, she finally glanced over at Alex. He sat there without any soup in his bowl. No, he had not finished it; he was not eating it! "Alex, why aren't you eating your soup" she choked out in a whisper.

"I don't eat that shit," he replied.

That was it. She was out of there, and thus began the checklist of minimum standards.

I agreed; even Sally CJ wouldn't eat the ingredients in that recipe. What was Jackie O thinking? The guy didn't even look good, and she surely didn't need the money. Must be a true verification that Greeks have the Big Salami.

If you haven't experienced the process of chemotherapy, it's definitely an activity that merits avoidance. Chemo means sitting in a Barcalounger in a room with a dozen scrawny, bald strangers for five hours while poison is injected into your body through a port in your chest. It looks like a feeding room from *Close Encounters of the Third Kind* or *The Matrix*. Now, your body doesn't like this poison in the least, so it fights it off. The prime fighting time is from midnight to 4:00 a.m. when the body goes into high gear and attempts to burn out the bad guys. All liquid seeps from the body, leaving fried deposits behind. Where does the fluid go? It creates a swamp in the bed.

At our first meeting, I asked Dr. Doom if we could have sex during chemo because I was afraid that chemo chemicals could get in my body (from any variety of entry routes), and I didn't want to suffer any side effects. He danced around the issue and told me that I had to be understanding and caring and that love was not dependent on sex. I thought he meant Graham wouldn't be able to find the Big Boy during chemo. Wrong, there's no sex during chemo because the cancer patient has to sleep on the floor since a princess does not sleep in a swamp.

This is what a

sleeps on:

Not this:

Being in a stable relationship is wonderful but also full of contradictions. Going from a person who was game for any attractive man with hair and good teeth to the feelings I now have is very frustrating. The realities of loving a cancer patient are eye opening. Of course we're talking about sex.

We finally came to a compromise to deal with the bed swamp. However, now I have a fundamental and potentially insurmountable problem. It's not the Big Boy. It's I, the woman of too many affairs to count on all my fingers and toes. I cannot cheat on Graham. What are you talking about? We're discussing sex with Graham. No, we're not. We're discussing sex with a Mexican hairless.

First, the man doesn't look like Graham. He's Jon-Luc Picard or Telly Savalas, depending on whether the hat is on or off. Quick solution, dark room and my sleep mask.

Next problem. The reach around and grab the butt doesn't work either because the butt is smooth as a baby's behind, not the furry bear my senses have become adjusted to. We're still trying to solve this one. We already discovered that sex stores do not sell ass wigs. Sex with a lamb's wool cloth covering his behind is not much better. Solutions are welcome.

We recently finished up the last chemo treatment, and Graham is in surgery to remove the tumor and associated lymph nodes. The surgeon estimated that the surgery will take over six hours. Marcia came to Vegas to keep me company, which has been a wonderful relief. I was going to go to the gym to kill time, but Marcia grimaced at the thought of me chatting it up with the boys while my husband is under the knife. We both are trying to lose a couple pounds, so the brewery was not an option either. We finally decided on the old female standby and were off to Nordstrom's.

It was as if the Gods were thinking of me. It was the first day of Nordstrom's semiannual women's sale. Two pairs of Ferragamo shoes, a matching purse, a couple bras and panties (no thongs), a St. John jacket, and it was time to go back to the hospital and wait.

Good thing the hospital was across the street from the Tenaya Creek Brewery. You really can work up a thirst while shopping. I even called one of my softball friends to join us for the wait. Pansy was playing the quarter slots and had three aces and the kicker. All she needed was another ace, and it was going to be a $250 payoff. Marcia had reverted to her old high school cheerleading days and was jumping around like a fool yelling, "Give me an ace!"

The afternoon crowd sitting around the bar was staring at us like we were having a coke high.

I offered the ultimate motivation. "Get the fourth ace, and I'll suck your toe!" I encouraged Pansy the best way I knew. There was silence in the bar, and then …

"Hot shit! You're fucked! Don't move. I'll be right back. I'm going to wash my foot." And with that, Pansy jumped up and ran across the bar.

I looked, and there was the fourth ace.

Pansy was hauling ass to the ladies' room, and everyone was waiting for me to bolt. Marcia had her purse in hand and was standing by the door.

"A promise is a promise," I muttered and knelt down, waiting for the starlet to emerge from the wash. There was a growing crowd around the video poker machine.

Pansy came hopping out of the ladies' room with a paper towel wrapped around her left foot. She sat on the stool, thrust her shoulders back, raised her leg, and pointed her toe.

I leaned over and instantly got caught up in the spirit of the cheering crowd, led by Marcia, who was standing on the bar. I took a deep breath and opened mouth, inserted foot.

We got back to the hospital, and Graham was still under the knife.

The four of us went to Hawaii six months after the funeral. It was horrible. I never felt so alone in my entire life. Even with the girls keeping close watch, I just couldn't get my act together.

One thing that was truly amazing was that the son who had caused massive amounts of gray hair and almost drove Graham and me apart during his teenage years less than ten years earlier was one of my sources of greatest comfort. It helped, but I just couldn't get out of the funk.

That was when Sally CJ, Frances, and Marcia decided it was time for me to quit sulking and get back into action. Marcia and Steve had a friend who owned a house on the Big Island, and before I knew it, we were drinking pina coladas on the back porch of a house right out of *Architecture Digest* that had a breathtaking view of the Kohala Coast.

I don't remember how to date. I had been married to Graham for sixteen years and had given up the thought of other men. "It's been over seventeen years since my last bar pick-up, and I was a size eight at that time," I whined.

"Now you know what we've been going through for years," bitched Sally CJ.

"The men don't know the difference between a size eight and a size twelve," explained Frances. "That's just bull shit from your days of bulimia. Your mother had the most warped view of proper body size. Do you remember how she went ape shit when you gained seventy-two pounds when you were pregnant? Just remember our saying, Get Over It! Blow jobs instantly melt away the pounds in the number-one brain."

Frances, the bitch, just sat there. If she moans that she can't fit in her size four Versace jeans one more time, Sally CJ is going to send her to China on the next wave.

"Just remember, the way to a man's heart is through his number-one brain," encouraged Sally CJ. I think Sally CJ has opened a franchise for Pansy's pleasure business on the East Coast.

"Yeah, remember what you did to your friend's toe that day in the bar?"

The girls froze and stared at Marcia in horror.

Rather than break down into hysterics, I laughed. "Yeah, even Pansy didn't think I would go through with it!"

We then began to develop a set of guidelines to ease me back into the dating game. Marcia sarcastically gave her input, "Dating at our age is like looking for a toilet in a public bathroom at the beach. You just try to pick out the cleanest one." How encouraging. With much effort, the sharks developed the following pointers for women who no longer have tiny waists and perky breasts and are reentering the dating scene:

1. Sex is good when it lasts longer than the commercial during a timeout on Monday Night Football.

2. While there might be such a thing as a "three dog night," there is no such thing as a "three orgasm night."

3. Do not eat spicy food before sex. There is much greater elasticity in the lower intestine, and farting is not a good way to sustain an erection.

4. Dating is to be fun and not result in serious complications. You need to conduct a very careful preliminary screening. Therefore, do not date a guy:

    a. Who still lives at home with his mother.

    b. Who is still paying child support or alimony unless his net worth is in terms of seven digits.

    c. You met at the release door to the county jail.

    d. Who hangs around homeless shelters, the INS, or a downtown mission.

    e. Who is not a lawyer but has an in-depth knowledge of the court system and is on a first-name basis with most of the judges.

    f. Who wears white socks with his Birkenstocks.

5. Where a guy hangs out is indicative of his pocketbook and your dating satisfaction. You no longer go to bars to meet a guy. You cannot compete with the young chicks and implants. Good places to meet a guy are:

    a. Investment and retirement seminars

    b. Golf courses

    c. First-class cabin on airplanes

6. A man on a first-name basis with the staff at Home Depot makes an excellent date.

7. A woman should never be on top after the age of fifty.

8. Do not have sex in the daylight unless the date is blind or you convinced him to have masquerade sex and wear a blindfold.

9. Do not date a guy wearing a Speedo even if he drives a Porsche.

10. A guy who wears socks to bed does not get a second date unless he has a twelve-inch dick.

The golden rule for sex after fifty is me first. This means that you coming first is a condition for male ejaculation.

With my courage up, we headed to the local pub, which fortunately served Guinness on draft. The place was packed, and we started scouting for a table.

It's amazing. Sally CJ must give off some kind of mating scent because within five minutes, this athletic guy in his midfifties, wearing a San Francisco 49ers baseball cap, walked up to her and asked if we wanted to join him and his pals for a drink.

Cool. It was easy. The guys were a real hoot. Two were lawyers. The stud in the baseball cap worked for the 49ers. Another guy was a retired soccer player who was into sports management, and I don't remember what Jim and Jack did. I have not laughed so hard in years.

Frances and I agreed to meet the lawyers for golf on Friday. I was actually smiling and wondering what I would do if the golf outing turned out so well the blond guy would want to get me in the sack. What if he wasn't interested? That would be even worse.

"Mrs. Jones. Wake up. Your husband is in the recovery room and is doing just fine. You can go up to his room as soon as he's awake."

I looked up, and there was Dr. Farley looking down at me.

"Are you okay?" he asked.

"You have no idea," I sighed. Thank God the dating game is not in my imminent future.

What's most upsetting about the past three months is the fact that I'm realizing that I've become monogamous. I guess it's good, but am I really growing up at fifty-five?

Sally CJ is planning a visit in a couple weeks to protect her future husband and to investigate Harris at the gym. Frances is investing in wine futures and is about to try the Internet dating game again. Marcia is falling in love and has decided that abstinence does not make the heart grow fonder.

I looked up, and Dr. Farley was still standing in front of me with his arms crossed. "Mrs. Jones, we still need to talk about the next steps for your husband's treatment. You can schedule an appointment with Dr. Dinacopoulous in ten days."

Well, I guess life is a bit better, at least for the moment.

The roses, the lovely notes, the dining and dancing are all welcome and splendid. But when the Godiva is gone, the gift of real love is having someone who'll go the distance with you. Someone who, when the wedding day limo breaks down, is willing to share a seat on the bus.

—Oprah Winfrey

Acknowledgments

I want to thank all of my friends who have had the patience to put up with me writing this book and for the many colorful stories that they shared to help develop the characters. I want to give special thanks to Kate, Nan, and Steve for their editing assistance. The book would not so perfectly reflect the Menopausal Killer Sharks without the wonderful illustrations by Emily Atkinson. Thank you, all.

Most of all, I want to thank my deceased husband, Colin, for encouraging me to write this story and for sixteen wonderful years of marriage.

Want to read about more adventures of the Sharks and laugh at their latest challenges in aging and dating?

They will broaden their horizons on a trip to Europe. Marcia will learn a lot more about what she really wants in a man; Laurie gets terrible news and a new neighbor; Sally CJ continues her poor behavior in a new job; Frances strikes a partnership with an outlandish Count. Check my website - janatkinsonbooks.com - for upcoming information on the sequel - "Shark Attack, The Girls are Back".